# CHRISTMAS ON BLUEBERRY BAY

## BLUEBERRY BAY

ELLEN JOY

Copyright © 2024 by Ellen Joy Author

All rights reserved.

No part of this book may be reproduced in any form or by any electronic or mechanical means, including information storage and retrieval systems, without written permission from the author, except for the use of brief quotations in a book review.

*To all my sports moms. Thanks for all your support over the years.*

Click HERE or visit ellenjoyauthor.com for more information about all of Ellen's books.

Cliffside Point
Beach Home Beginnings
Seaview Cottage
Sugar Beach Sunsets
Home on the Harbor
Christmas at Cliffside
Lakeside Lighthouse
Seagrass Sunrise
Half Moon Harbor
Seashell Summer
Beach Home Dreams

Camden Cove
The Inn by the Cove
The Farmhouse by the Cove
The Restaurant by the Cove
The Christmas Cottage by the Cove
The Bakery by the Cove

Prairie Valley Sisters
Coming Home to the Valley
Daydreams in the Valley
Starting Over in the Valley
Second Chances in the Valley
New Hopes in the Valley
Feeling Blessed in the Valley

Blueberry Bay
The Cottage on Blueberry Bay
The Market on Blueberry Bay

The Lighthouse on Blueberry Bay
The Fabric Shop on Blueberry Bay
Christmas on Blueberry Bay

Beach Rose Secrets

# CHAPTER 1

Stephanie flattened out her skirt with her hands as she waited for her interview. She sat in the front hall of the Abbott house, waiting for her appointment with the current house manager. She and another woman were silent as they waited, and she wondered if they ever decorated for Christmas or if things were just running late this year, considering they were hiring a new house manager.

Janet, the current manager, had been here for as long as Stephanie could remember. She hoped Janet had started working for the Abbotts in her twenties as well, and then maybe the age difference between the woman waiting for an interview wouldn't matter. Stephanie recognized the woman but couldn't place her.

"You grew up in Blueberry Bay, right?" Stephanie asked, unable to sit in the silence any longer. "I'm Stephanie LaBelle."

"I know," the woman said flatly. "I'm Lyndsey O'Malley—well, Sullivan now. I went to high school with your brother, Will."

Five years older, Stephanie noted in her head. Five years more experience than Stephanie had. She couldn't help but glance over at Lyndsey again. She hadn't aged too well for only being in her early thirties.

"This house is even bigger than it looks across the bay."

Stephanie glanced around the front hall, which her family's house would fit inside. If she lived here, she'd have a towering Christmas tree standing in the middle of the curved staircase that swept up to the second floor. She'd have garland and lights wrapping around the wooden banister all the way to the second-floor balcony.

"Yeah," Lyndsey mumbled, then immediately went back to her phone.

Stephanie wanted to get up and check out the things around the room. The whole space screamed old money, but most tastefully and beautifully. From the curved staircase that stole everyone's attention against the far end of the room to the gilded-framed oil paintings to the antique furniture, it was everything she had dreamt of all these years living across the bay, wondering what the big beautiful house on the cliffs of the Atlantic Ocean would look like inside.

As a little girl, Stephanie had stared over Blueberry Bay's waters at the large white colonial house. She'd dreamed of someday living there, having one of the Abbott grandsons fall madly in love with her. The house had been built over a century ago and had the classic New England style like the Kennedys' houses built on the Cape or the Bushes' in Kennebunkport. It was large enough to be considered a mansion but elegant and moderately extended, with smooth, clean lines that made the house dignified, not gaudy and showy.

Sitting in a chair that probably cost more than her monthly salary at the diner, she wished she could raise a family in a place so beautiful. How did the rich get their money anyway? She had heard the Abbott family did something in politics and banking and had more money than she'd ever seen in her lifetime. But seriously, how does one get to be this rich?

The front room doors opened, and an elderly woman walked a young woman out—younger than her, Stephanie guessed.

"I'll let you know when we make our final decision, but it should be within a day or two."

They shook hands and both women walked out. When the older one returned, she said, "Lyndsey Sullivan. My goodness, you look great!"

Lyndsey, who'd had a scowl the whole time sitting there, now smiled wide and hugged the older woman. "It's good to see you too, Aunt Janet."

*Great*, thought Stephanie.

She had no experience as a "house manager." She didn't know what a house manager even did. The only reason she'd considered it was the benefits she'd receive. But now, seeing there was competition, she probably shouldn't waste anyone's time. Mostly hers. She could run down to the coffee shop and have a quiet cup of coffee by herself, which sounded just as dreamy as a paid holiday. What made her think she'd be qualified to work here? She was only a waitress, according to her resume.

Just as she was about to get up and sneak out, the front door opened, and a man walked into the house. Stephanie looked up and recognized him right away.

Julian Abbott.

He, too, was the same age as her brother. She wondered if he would even remember the fact that they had played on the beaches together as kids. Probably not. The rich summer kids usually forgot about the local kids by the time they figured out their differences. It usually happened in high school. Their preparatory and private schools helped establish their perceived superiority over the lower townsfolk.

"Hey," he said, making eye contact with her as he strolled through the room.

She wasn't expecting him to say hey or even acknowledge her. She certainly wasn't going to acknowledge him. She looked around to ensure he wasn't saying it to someone else. Did he remember her? "Hey."

"Can I get you anything while you wait?" he asked.

She suddenly felt awkward and uncomfortable. Should she get up and shake his hand or curtsy? She stayed put.

3

"Nope." She shook her head and smiled at him. He smiled back. Maybe he did remember her. She still couldn't hide her surprise at his hospitality. She thought about the last time she'd seen him. He had crashed a party of a friend of hers and drank everyone's drinks. That had to be six years ago, at least. Before Asher was born—it was at least six years. "I'm good, but thanks."

"Sure." He gave her a nod.

Stephanie couldn't help but let her eyes follow as he left the room. Julian Abbott had been legendary among the women in Blueberry Bay. Everyone had chased after him—even the older women. And from what Stephanie had heard over the years, he had chased everyone, except Stephanie.

Soon, the doors to the front hall opened, and Lyndsey left the office.

"Stephanie," Janet said with a smile. "I didn't know you were considering getting a new job." She waited until Lyndsey walked out the front doors to embrace Stephanie. "How are you doing, my dear?"

"I'm fine," Stephanie said. She had known Janet all her life, but clearly not as well as Lyndsey.

Janet led her through the double doors into a large room. The beige walls had more gilded-framed paintings—large oil paintings, mostly of ocean landscapes, but also some portraits.

"How's Asher?" Janet asked toward a gorgeous walnut desk with skinny carved legs and a large, even more elaborately carved top.

"Great. He's getting so big," Stephanie said. *Too big.*

"Is he in school yet?" Janet asked, pointing to the chair to indicate where Stephanie should sit.

Stephanie sat down as instructed. "He just started first grade."

"Wow, already? Geez." Janet shook her head as she sat down, tapping a computer screen awake. "Time flies. I remember when you and Gabe got married."

Stephanie sat quietly, hoping the topic of Gabe would end.

"Yes, well, let's get to it, shall we?" Janet said. "Do you have any experience working as a house manager?"

Stephanie wondered if *house manager* was the politically correct way of saying *maid*. "No, I do not. But I have worked all over town, as you know, and you can ask anyone about my work ethic. I'm a hard worker and eager to learn."

Stephanie sat up straighter, hoping that would make her look more like house manager material.

"It's not just cleaning and cooking; it's being a caretaker of this house," Janet said, holding up her hands. "You're the curator of this house, and it's like a museum, with priceless artifacts important to the Abbotts' legacy, our town and state, and even our country! Do you think you can take care of something like this?"

"Well, I've kept Asher alive," Stephanie joked, but it didn't seem to land with Janet.

She smiled at Stephanie and continued with the interview.

"How are your social skills?" Janet asked.

"Excuse me?" Stephanie wasn't expecting that kind of question. Another joke flashed in her head, but Janet started talking before she could come up with a professional answer.

"You'll be asked to greet and serve some of the most influential people in New England and around the world." Janet's eyebrows lifted like she was making sure Stephanie was paying attention.

"Well, I serve all kinds of people at the diner."

Janet wrote something down on a notepad.

"I was valedictorian of my high school graduating class and spoke at the ceremony," Stephanie reminded Janet. "I also did a very short stint as an administrative assistant at a law office, greeting clients, answering phones, scheduling meetings, and assisting the shareholders in any way I could."

She used all the keywords she could think of at the top of her head. Before Asher, she had thought she'd want to attend medical school, but medical school had to be suspended when she got pregnant.

"That's right. I forgot you were a smart cookie." Janet pointed her pencil at Stephanie. "Good. That's a good thing. Mr. Abbott likes intelligent staff."

"Does he live here all year?" Stephanie asked.

Janet shook her head. "No, most of the winter Mr. Abbott travels to his other house in Florida, but he will return for holidays with the boys."

An image of Julian Abbott's backside flashed in her mind. "Great."

"However, as of recently, there has been someone living here." Janet looked over Stephanie's shoulder as she said it. "Oliver, his grandson, lived here until his wedding. Now his brother, Julian, has been staying here."

"Julian Abbott's been living in Blueberry Bay?" It wasn't summer, but almost Christmas.

Janet nodded. "For almost a year."

What was Julian Abbott doing living in Blueberry Bay?

*Hiding*, she quickly thought to herself but took it back. She didn't see a ring on his finger, which didn't necessarily mean anything. He could get any woman with that chiseled jawline and bank account. Why stick around in Blueberry Bay all winter?

"I haven't seen him at all around town," Stephanie said, surprised by this. She would have heard something at the diner. During the summer months, she'd listen to gossip about him all the time while working at the diner, through friends, and even from her mother's friends gossiping. Julian Abbott, the most eligible bachelor in New England, always seemed to be with the next beautiful woman and out in the small village, causing havoc.

Maybe in high school that kind of behavior would seem exciting and dangerous, but as a single mom raising a son alone, she'd rather live with her father for the rest of her life than with someone like that again.

Janet went through some other questions, which further

6

showcased how little experience Stephanie had with house-keeping and managing a house.

"Do you have any questions for me?" Janet asked, finished with hers.

Stephanie had read somewhere that you should have three questions about the job itself and not its benefits, but that's the only reason Stephanie wanted to work as a house manager. "The job comes with medical and dental. Is that true?"

Janet nodded. "Yes, that's right."

A huge step up from the diner.

"And paid holidays and sick days?" She bit her bottom lip, hoping this one was true as well.

Janet nodded. "The first year you will have eight, then one day more the next, and so forth."

Stephanie quickly added up the days in her head after five years, then ten years, then how many if she reached Janet's age.

"Working for the Abbotts, you will get paid time off, but it has to be requested and not just any old day. You can call in sick, but they need someone reliable, well-organized, and professional."

"Yes, of course." Stephanie doubted she fit Janet's expectations.

Stephanie needed another question that didn't have to do with the perks. She threw in, "How many guests tend to stay during the year?"

Janet shifted her position, pencil ready to write down anything Stephanie said. "Tell me, Stephanie. Why did you apply?"

Wow, straight to the point. Stephanie could tell a story and make it sound like she dreamed of becoming a house manager, but she also decided to get to the point. No need to hide her true feelings. "I need a reliable paycheck for me and my family."

This made Janet nod.

"How's Gabe doing?" Janet asked, probably not knowing about the divorce.

Stephanie didn't talk about it, even though it'd been over a year. Not that anyone would know the difference, since Gabe had always been deployed or just chasing after other women.

"He's good. Living in Portland now," Stephanie said.

Janet's eyebrows raised immediately. "Still in the Navy?"

Stephanie shook her head. "No, not anymore."

Janet nodded. And Stephanie knew Janet wanted to ask more questions but held back to be polite. Who wouldn't want to ask why the valedictorian and football captain had broken up? They had been together since they were kids. Everyone had expected them to work out.

"We divorced," Stephanie said, not sure why. She didn't usually talk about it with anyone.

Janet made a face as though it were bad news. "I'm sorry to hear that. You two were so cute together when you won homecoming king and queen."

People still thought they were that couple. The couple who had big dreams together. The couple who loved each other. The couple who said they'd do anything for each other. Not the couple who hardly saw or spoke to each other when they were together. Not the couple that had nothing in common. Not the couple who stayed together because of their son. Not that couple.

"That feels like forever ago," Stephanie said, and it did.

"How's your dad?" Janet asked, changing the subject.

That's when Stephanie knew she hadn't gotten the job. Janet didn't go back to the interview. After a brief conversation about her family and what her siblings were up to, Janet thanked Stephanie for coming.

"I appreciate your time," Stephanie said as they walked out. No one else was waiting for an interview.

"I'll let you know when I schedule a second round of interviews," Janet said, escorting her out.

"That would be great, thanks." Stephanie gave a small wave and looked back into the hall, wishing she could ask Janet for a tour. "It's such a pretty house."

Janet smiled, looking around the room. "Yes, The Abbotts have really taken care of this place."

"When I was a little girl," Stephanie confessed, looking around the room one last time, "I used to daydream about what this place would look like inside, and it's completely met my expectations."

That's when, out of the corner of her eye, she saw someone standing in the doorway. Julian stood just far enough back beyond the doorframe that she couldn't see him at first, but as she turned, he came into view.

With a slight jerk, she straightened and gave him a wave. "Thanks for your time."

She gave Janet a strange half curtsy and left the doors open. As she walked to where she had parked, she couldn't help but look back at the house to the front doors, and just as she did, she met eyes with Julian Abbott.

# CHAPTER 2

"*I*s that Stephanie?" he asked, wondering if he got that right. He used to hang out with her brother. "Her brother's Will, right?"

Janet nodded, walking into the formal dining room and pulling out some dishes from a glass cabinet.

"Yes, you used to practically live at the LaBelle's house," Janet answered, busy at work. "You remember little Stephie?"

Julian nodded. Janet would remember more than he would, he supposed. She had been the one supervising them most of the time. Not his parents. That was almost comical. If they had been watching the kids, they'd most definitely had a drink with them and were in no shape to be in charge of children. His grandfather would allow the grandchildren to stay and eat with him, but the house was his leisure zone. That meant he wanted a lot of alone time. Small rambunctious children didn't fit into that leisure time except when it came to golf, fishing, or going out on the boat, which was less and less by the time Julian had come around.

"She's applying for your position?" He hadn't expected someone so young to fill Janet's spot. He expected another gray-haired Janet.

Janet shook her head. "I've got a few other candidates that will be a better fit."

"Why not Stephanie?" he asked, surprised.

From what Julian remembered, Stephanie had always been a nice girl whenever he'd hung out with her brother. He had always enjoyed Will's family and secretly envied their big family in the small house. Everyone was in everyone else's business, there was no privacy, and it was always loud. He loved it.

Growing up as an Abbott was the opposite. Everyone held secrets in his family. They were isolated in their big houses, hardly saw one another, and when they were together, they hardly talked to one another. When he did talk to his parents, they chastised him for his choices and how he lacked ambition. He didn't talk much to his sister, only Oliver—who was so busy being a newlywed he didn't have much time.

He could not blame his brother for wanting to live his new life with his beautiful bride. He shouldn't have to worry about his little brother anymore.

Another one of Julian's problems was that everyone had taken care of him. He'd never had to grow up and deal with things himself. What a waste. Years of just living in automatic forward without even so much as a why. Why did he want to work in finance? Why did he go to the same prep school as his father and the same college and go into the same industry? For what? To become the same miserable man that his father had always been? His grandfather may have had a reckoning when his grand-mother died five years ago, but he had cranked the wheel in the cog for so long that the damage had been done.

Thank goodness for Oliver; otherwise, Julian wouldn't have been sure what he would be doing now.

"Why?" he asked again. It might be nice to have someone younger to help around the house.

Janet furrowed her eyebrows and shrugged. "She has no experience." She crossed her arms. "Why so interested?"

Julian almost said something but stopped himself just in time.

The old Julian would have made an idiotic comment about the job being easy enough to figure out, or that anyone with half a brain could do the job, though he had no idea what it entailed. The old Julian would assume Janet hardly did anything besides clean and cook, because those are the things she did in front of him. He had never gone out of his way to find out what she did when he wasn't around.

"Are the LaBelles all still fishing?" he asked. He hadn't talked to Will in years. It was common for fishing families to continue in that line of work throughout the generations. Like an Abbott working in finance, politics, or law, your profession was chosen the second you were born.

Janet nodded. "Will's got his own boat now."

"Then she knows about hard work," he said, remembering the boys up and on the water before the sun rose.

"How long do you think your grandfather will live?" Janet asked so bluntly that it threw him off. He didn't like to think of his grandfather as someone who was approaching his time.

"He could live until he's a hundred," Julian said. It wasn't unheard of, and even being eighty-four, the old man still had a lot of life left in him. He golfed and fished and exercised.

"But if he doesn't"—Janet folded her hands together— "she'll lose her job and her benefits."

The power of the statement didn't hit Julian right away—until it did. "Does that mean the house will be sold?"

Janet nodded. "Your father doesn't want to keep this place."

"But somebody will?" Julian thought of his siblings. His sister didn't even live on the East Coast. "Oliver is never leaving Blueberry Bay."

His older sister never liked the house in Maine, deeming the temperature too cold for her. Oliver couldn't afford a house like his grandfather's on just a teacher's salary. The timeless beauty's taxes were probably close to his yearly salary. He couldn't afford it either, that was for sure. He didn't even have a job at this point.

"Have you talked to Will since you've been back?" Janet asked.

Julian shook his head. He hadn't kept in touch with Will over the years but hadn't really run into anyone since being back in Blueberry Bay.

"I should call Will," he said.

"Might be uncomfortable since I'm not calling his sister for a second interview," Janet said, carrying a huge porcelain dish to the kitchen.

"Can I help you?" Julian asked. "With the hiring?"

Janet stopped in her spot. "Julian Abbott, when have you ever asked to help me?"

"Have I been that bad all this time?" Julian should have known, but he hadn't thought of Janet as someone to help. As pathetic as it sounded, he hadn't known better.

"Yes." Janet was no longer worried about keeping her job if she upset the grandchildren, apparently.

He froze, not sure how to reply. "Right."

"I'm sorry." Janet put the dish onto the counter. "I don't mean to be harsh. I'd love to give Stephanie the job, and Lord knows she needs it. But the truth is, I can't hire someone like Stephanie when you two grown men living here haven't ever so much as picked up a dish on your own."

Julian looked at her, not sure what her point was.

"It's too big for one inexperienced house cleaner who won't be getting any help from you two." Janet shook her head.

"I wash dishes," he argued. But he had been a spoiled brat most of his life. Only recently had he opened his eyes to his self-indulgences and narcissism. He would be ashamed to admit this now, but at one point in his life, he had believed he was better than others just because of his family's name and money.

Now he wanted nothing to do with it.

"She's a local," he argued. "She wants to stay. Obviously, she's wicked smart. She could've made it somewhere, but she stayed."

She tsked her tongue as though she were talking to him like he was still a teenager. "She may be the prettiest, but she's the least qualified applicant."

Julian shook his head. "It's not like that."

He had enough problems with his love life. He wasn't looking to add to that mess.

"Speaking of which," Julian said as the doorbell rang at the front gates of the house. He looked at the camera, which showed Brandon Rossi pulling up.

Brandon came through the back door and hugged Janet as soon as he saw her. "I'm so glad you're still here."

"I'm not leaving just yet." Janet patted him on the back. "Glad to see you, too."

Like every Wednesday afternoon, Brandon got together with Julian. This ritual had started when Julian had gotten out of rehab. A fact he was still ashamed of even, though he knew he should be proud. However, no one, not even himself, thought he could make it alone. Hence, the reason why he lived with his grandfather near his brother and best friend and sponsor. He'd rather live in a city with a pulse and something to do rather than sit and rot away listening to the same waves, the same wind, the same birds, the same people day in and day out. Nothing changed in Blueberry Bay, including the people.

But that's what he needed right now to stay sober.

"Janet, what do you plan to do when you retire?" Brandon asked.

"I'm moving to Florida with my Frank." Janet clapped her hands together. "Can't wait. We're going to get a boat and drink margaritas all day." Janet winced. "Sorry boys. I forget…"

"That sounds great," Brandon said, waving away her worry. Like Julian, Brandon was in recovery, but unlike Julian, he had his life together.

Brandon turned to Julian, giving him a half handshake, half hug. "Hey, man, how's it going?"

"Good," Julian said, looking at the container in Brandon's hand. "What did you bring this time?"

Brandon gently shook the tin. "Gingerbread cookies."

"I'll get some coffee going," Janet said, knowing Julian would want coffee—his newest obsession since he stopped drinking.

"Thanks, Janet," Julian said, something he'd never done in the past, he realized.

"I'll be back, boys," Janet said, ushering them into the lounge, which, as kids, they'd called the TV room. The only room in the whole house that had one. His grandfather wouldn't allow it in any other room. The lounge had been the only room without a view of the great Atlantic Ocean.

"You want to take off instead?"

Brandon usually convinced Julian to leave the house for their meetings. They'd hike or walk down by the water. The house seemed to make Brandon uncomfortable, which Julian now understood. The longer he stayed sober, the more he became aware of things. Things he'd never noticed or had ignored. Like his family's money and how much they liked to flaunt it. The people who were attracted to it or repelled by it.

When he was a kid, he hadn't really paid attention to the other kids and how little they'd had compared to him. He'd known he had more than others but hadn't truly understood how much more.

Luckily, most people in Blueberry Bay didn't seem to care about their money. Or they pretended not to. As a kid, he'd been included in the community as though he were one of them. The bars had treated him like a local when he'd turned up at their establishments as an adult.

"It's too cold outside today." Julian sat on the couch and opened the cookie tin with a snowman on the cover. He passed it over to Brandon, who took a cookie.

"A number-one best-selling author and a pastry chef—where do you find the time?" Julian teased, but he admired Brandon's willingness to try anything and do anything. Julian hardly left the house.

"Muriel's mom, Meredith, is showing me how to bake in

exchange for me teaching her my mom's sauce and other family recipes," Brandon explained, taking a cookie himself.

"Sharing the secret family recipe." Julian shook his head, joking around. "How does Lucia feel about that?"

Brandon shrugged, biting off the head of the cookie. "Good. I mean, Cora's going to be family now."

And Julian bit down hard into his gingerbread man's leg. He'd be lying if he said it didn't sting a bit each time he heard how happy they were, even if he had pushed them together. How do you make someone as great as Cora wait around until you can get your head straight? If you even could. Because, at this stage in the game, a year of sobriety still hadn't cured him. The urge to drink was a very real and powerful thing for Julian.

So, he let her go.

Wasn't that a song by the Rolling Stones? Can't always get what you want? Julian certainly didn't get anything he wanted.

"How are you doing, really?" Brandon asked, leaning back in his spot.

Their afternoon chats were more of a counseling session. Brandon said he needed them as much as Julian, but Julian doubted it. Brandon had pulled his life together and turned into an overnight success. He'd just finished another novel he'd sent to his publisher and was working on a third. His career had taken off and the sky was the limit.

Julian's career had crashed and burned.

After his stint in rehab, returning to his old world hadn't worked. Like wearing an outgrown pair of shoes, he'd felt constricted and needed room. He wanted to grow and not return to the Julian he was before—the guy who had numbed his feelings by drinking.

"I'm good." Julian kept busy. If not, he'd fall into his imagination and relive all the horrible things he had done in the past, going over and over all his mistakes. And what he'd sadly come to realize was that the passing time didn't make him forget any of it.

They controlled his thoughts during the day, his conversations, and while he slept, they'd creep into his dreams. Everything he had done over the years, starting when he'd first drank at age thirteen. It sounded so young now.

"When did you first have a drink?" Julian asked Brandon.

Brandon rested his leg on his other knee, looking up to the ceiling as he thought back. "I think I was sixteen, besides a sip here and there with my dad."

Julian had sipped forever. By the time he'd had his first real drink at thirteen, he'd felt the effects of all those sips and was looking for more.

"My parents love to entertain." Julian looked at his watch. They'd be arriving in less than a month for Christmas. "I'm worried for when they get here."

"I thought they've been supportive," Brandon said.

Julian had to give it to his parents. Initially, they had been supportive. Even his mother had stopped drinking her afternoon apéritifs in front of him. But that's not what he was most concerned about.

"I haven't been around my father—sober—since I was..." He hated thinking these truths. "I started drinking."

Steven Abbott had never understood his youngest child. He had been supportive when Julian cleaned up, but the aftermath had strained their relationship even more than it already had been. His father didn't understand why Julian had quit his job. He didn't understand why Julian would want to get away from his old life. And he certainly didn't like Julian's change in perspective. He thought he needed to toughen up and get on with it. Definitely not sit around eating gingerbread cookies, drinking coffee, and talking about feelings.

"I think I'll need to leave at that point," Julian said. "Go back to the city."

"Really?" Brandon cocked his head. "I thought you were going to teach me how to winter surf."

"Oliver will teach you," Julian said. "I'll come back."

Brandon's eyebrows lifted. "You seem to do so well here."

"I do," he said honestly. "It's just my dad. I don't know what it is, but the two of us have always been like oil and water."

"Ah." Brandon nodded. "What about Oliver? Do they get along?"

"Yes and no." Julian shrugged. "They have their own complicated relationship."

"Do you think leaving is the right thing to do?" Brandon asked, pushing Julian, like always, to say more. "Don't you want to build a new relationship with your dad, being sober?"

"I don't think there is a relationship," Julian said. "Doesn't Father Michael always talk about letting go and setting up boundaries so we can keep our sobriety? I think this relationship is best from a distance. Over the phone. Email. I don't know. But definitely not living under the same roof."

"How long are they staying?" Brandon asked.

"I don't know. Sometimes it's a week, sometimes longer. Sometimes, he just shows up. I don't want to worry about him coming."

"Do you want to go back to the city?" Brandon asked.

Julian leaned back, exhaling out a long breath, thinking about that one. "Not really. But I think I'm ready for a change. I can't stay in this house much longer."

Brandon shook his head as he leaned over to the table and grabbed another cookie. "I don't know, man. I'm trying to get my family to move up here. There's something about hearing the waves and smelling the sea that just makes life ...peaceful."

Julian wanted that peace, but he felt that being in love with a woman like Cora added to Brandon's bliss. "My dad wants me to return to my old Diversified Business and Credit job."

The commercial loan company had been his father's most significant investment and Julian's last employer. When he'd entered rehab, they had spun the narrative that Julian was taking a year's sabbatical. He'd expected his father to ask him to resign quietly, but now his father wanted him to come back.

Julian wondered what his life would be like if he had been

taught how to drink responsibly or been told the devastating effects alcohol would have on him and his body. Maybe he wouldn't have started drinking at all.

But his life had been filled with alcohol. Every night, drinks were served at dinner. Weekends started with mimosas and Bloody Marys. Holidays had special drinks catered to the festivities. Even a normal lunch out would include a glass of wine or a gin and tonic. His father always had a beer during a round of golf and after working out. Alcohol was as much a part of his life as his family was.

And he didn't want to live like that anymore.

Janet entered the room with a tray of scones she had made.

"These look great, Janet," Brandon said.

"Only a few more weeks of my blueberry scones," she said.

"When is your grandfather returning?" Brandon asked.

"Mr. Abbott's returning on the fourth," Janet answered for Julian. "Just in time for this one's birthday."

Brandon smiled mischievously. "You didn't tell me your birthday was coming up."

Julian shook his head, wishing Janet hadn't said anything. "I'm not big into birthdays."

"Well, that's no fun," Brandon said. He looked at Janet. "I think we should have a birthday celebration for our dear friend Julian. Don't you, Janet?" Brandon's eyes widened in delight.

Julian dreaded the thought of Brandon planning something. "I'm cool not doing anything."

"How old are you going to be?" Brandon asked, talking to Julian like he was turning five years old.

Janet played along. "This one's turning the big three oh."

Brandon's mouth widened at the news. "You're turning thirty!"

Julian wished it weren't true. He had already wasted thirty years, and what did he have to show for it? He had a bleeding bank account, no job, and was completely starting over with not only his career but also his home, his friends, and everything he knew.

And now he was thirty.

"Sure am," he said, pouring his coffee. If only his father could see him now. "Want a delicious cookie Brandon made?"

He lifted the tin to Janet, who peeked inside and then looked admiringly at Brandon. "You baked these yourself?"

"Well, Meredith helped," Brandon said humbly, as always. The guy was a saint compared to an Abbott.

Janet took one and held it up in the air. "Thank you."

Brandon gave her a nod as she left them to themselves.

"Are you getting a new Janet?" Brandon asked.

Julian set his mug down, getting up from the chair. "They're looking for someone as we speak."

He thought about Stephanie and hoped she wasn't counting on the job. He walked toward the bookshelf filled with hundreds, if not thousands, of books, all of which had been read over the last century by various family members. He pulled the spine of a book he had told Brandon about. A French classic his mother had to read when she was in grammar school, *Le Père Goriot* by Honoré de Balzac. A story that showcased life in the nineteenth century of Paris.

"Finding someone like Janet is going to be a tall order," Brandon said, drinking his coffee. "She makes really good coffee."

Julian nodded, handing over the book. "My mother had to read this in school."

Brandon looked at the spine. "It's all in French?"

Julian nodded. "You know enough to read *Les Misérables*."

"With a full class and a professor to help me through it." Brandon held the thick text in his hands. He flipped through the pages and looked at the margins. "Is this your mother's writing?"

Julian nodded. Before his mother had become Mrs. Steven Abbott, Geneviève Aubert had left Paris for the London ballet, only to marry a man from Boston and never dance again. Yet, she raised a family—most very successful. She was a great mother who loved her children with passion, yet she could also be cold and distant. If he could self-diagnose her, he'd say she was depressed, but maybe he projected his own feelings.

He clearly had mommy issues, looking at the way he dated woman after woman, never letting them in, never getting to know them. Instead, he had paraded women in and out, not caring how he made them feel. All he cared about was himself, himself, himself.

The two sat and talked more about books, life, and the challenges they faced with being sober. Julian always felt better after these talks with Brandon, but the monkey on his back never left.

"Thanks for the book." Brandon lifted it at Julian as he prepared to leave.

"Anytime," Julian said, getting out of his chair to walk Brandon out. "Next Wednesday?"

"Let's go hiking," Brandon said. "The forecast doesn't look so bad next week."

Julian hoped so. "It's been cold for a long time already."

The winter looked bleak, considering it was only December.

Brandon nodded. "I thought Boston's winter was early."

Julian looked at the bare branches outside on the gray cloudy day. "I'd like to see some sun at some point."

Brandon left as Janet walked back into the kitchen.

"I made a beef roast," she said, pointing to a cast iron pot on the stove. "It's ready to eat when you are."

"It smells delicious." Julian remembered what she had said about Stephanie. "Thanks."

"It's my job," Janet said, picking up her coat. "I'll see you tomorrow."

"See you tomorrow," Julian said, but he stopped her before she reached the door. "It's none of my business, but what did you mean about Stephanie needing the job so badly? Is she okay?"

It had bothered him all afternoon. The way Janet had said it made him think something bigger was going on.

"She has a six-year-old she needs to care for," Janet said.

This surprised Julian. Little Stephanie was a mother? He did the math in his head. Stephanie had to be twenty-six. Young to be a mother, or at least in his world, which he was learning, was a very small world. Maybe in Blueberry Bay people got married and had families young.

"She just got divorced, too, which doesn't help." Janet lowered her voice as if they weren't the only two people in the house. "Gabe Turner took off and left her to raise a six-year-old all by herself."

"That's horrible," he said. "Seems like she has a good reason to take the job seriously."

Janet nodded. "Yes, I suppose so."

"What if I start helping more with taking care of my things while I stay here?" he asked, not sure why he'd gotten involved in the first place.

Janet stood there, not saying a word but just blinking at him. Then, after a long moment of awkward silence, she asked, "Do you have a thing for this girl?"

"No!" he said quickly. "I just feel bad for her, that's all. She looked excited for the job."

"If she doesn't work out, I won't be here to help, and your grandfather isn't always the easiest to please."

Julian had come to learn a lot about their family over the past year. When he'd entered rehab, therapy was mandatory. Session after session, the more Julian learned about himself, the more he learned about his dysfunctional family.

With all the wealth his family had accumulated over the years, and continued to accumulate, he'd have to be blind not to notice they hardly gave back or did any philanthropy for the greater good. They would put their names on charity events, buy seats at the elite tables, get their name on a plaque in a new wing, but never for the greater good. All for name recognition, marketing, schmoozing, and, worst of all, bragging rights.

Their newest attention grab to combat the bad press about their youngest son going into rehab was to "get involved" in the rehabilitation business. His father saw nothing but growth and opportunities to "help" others like his son. Before Julian had left the center he'd stayed at for his own rehabilitation, his father had started investing.

Maybe it was time he did some good and helped this single mother.

Would Father Michael be proud of him?

"You sure you can't try her out?" he said, hoping she might change her mind.

"I'm sure," Janet said, walking out of the house without looking back.

# CHAPTER 3

Stephanie hadn't thought she really even wanted the job until she put Asher to bed.

"Do you think Santa's going to get my list in time?" he asked as she pulled his covers up to his chin.

"Yes," she said. The panic of Christmas twisted her stomach. Unfortunately, customers in Blueberry Bay during the holiday season were not much into the giving spirit with their tips. If anything, they were like Stephanie and tightened their wallets. She had half of what she needed for Asher's list.

She couldn't believe she hadn't received a call. How could she not be hired over someone like Lyndsey O'Malley, who her brother said had barely made it out of high school?

She had resigned herself to the fact that she wouldn't get the call, so at breakfast the next morning, when her dad answered the phone and said it was Julian Abbott, she ignored him at first.

"It's Julian Abbott for you," her dad said, holding out the old family landline.

"For me?" Why would Julian Abbott call her? Wouldn't Janet be calling her about the job? She took the phone in her hand and walked to the wall where it had hung since before her parents had moved into her grandparents' house. "Hello?"

"Stephanie?" Julian sounded surprised by her voice.

"Yes?"

"I hope this isn't a bad time," he said.

"No, it's fine," she said, but she had maybe three minutes before the morning chaos would ensue. Asher would need to catch the bus, which was the most challenging part of her day. It may have been three months since school had started, but he still had breakdowns before leaving for school every day.

"I'm calling about the house manager position," he said in a monotone voice. She couldn't read it.

"Yes...?" she dragged out as an unbearable silence came from his end of the line.

"I'm calling to set up a trial run, two weeks, if possible," he said.

Her stomach dropped. "A trial during the holidays?"

That wouldn't work. She couldn't tell Lindy she was leaving for two weeks during the busiest time of the year to work at a job that *might* hire her.

"You have no experience," he said, as though that was a good enough answer to trial someone's livelihood.

"Yeah, thanks, but I will have to pass." She had one minute before she had to get Asher to the bus. "I appreciate the offer."

"But you're not going to take it?" he asked, surprised.

"Um...no..." She didn't know what he wanted her to say. "Thanks, but I can't miss two weeks of work for a trial run."

"Aren't you a waitress?" he asked, in a tone that suggested her job was meaningless and that she should be thanking him for giving her the two weeks.

And she would not. The scrappy fisherman's daughter brewed in annoyance that she'd spent her night wishing to be good enough for someone like him.

"I may not have the *experience* working as a house manager, Mr. Abbott, but I run my household, which includes taking care of my family." Wouldn't being a playboy bachelor living off Daddy's wealth be nice? She may live in her dad's household, but she had been running it since her mother passed away three years ago, and she never got a dime for her work. "Thanks again for the offer."

She hung up, and it felt good.

She walked away as her father came into the kitchen, lifting his eyebrows as if waiting for her to say something.

"I need to get Asher to the bus," she said, looking at the time. She walked toward the hallway when the phone rang again.

"Hello?" her father said. He'd stood in the kitchen to overhear her earlier conversation. "Sure, she's right here."

He held out the phone to her.

She shook her head. "I'm not available right now. Take a message."

Without looking back, she went to Asher's room, ignoring what her father said on the phone. She opened Asher's door. As she walked into the dark room, she hoped a permanent morning shift at the diner would open up so she wouldn't have to work so many nights. She could try to find a different full-time job, but not in Blueberry Bay. She'd been looking for years. She'd be stuck making minimum wage.

"Hey, little man," she said. She sat on his bed, instantly snuggling up against his warm, squishable body.

Fully dressed, Asher had snuck back under his covers.

"Dude, we just made the bed," she whispered as she leaned her cheek against his head, inhaling the scent his hair, wishing she could bottle it up before he grew out of it, or she couldn't sniff him any longer.

She wondered if Gabe even knew his son's scent.

"It's time to go to school," she whispered.

"No…" Asher whined. "I don't want to go to school."

And so, Stephanie's morning began. The daily argument about leaving her commenced.

"You love Mrs. Merrill," Stephanie reminded him. Asher loved school. Just not until she left, and the tears dried up.

"I don't want to go," he whimpered. The tears were already

forming. His bottom lip glistened with spit. "I want to stay here with you."

"Mommy has to work," she said. "Tonight, we get to have dinner together."

"Can we have McDonald's?" he asked excitedly.

His frown returned when she shook her head. "No, that's Uncle Will's thing."

"You promise you'll be home for dinner?" Asher asked, his body pressing against her even more.

"Of course I'm going to be here," she said, wrapping her arm around him and squeezing him tight. But she couldn't blame him for being scared that she might not return. His father took off every chance he could, using the Navy as his excuse for his absence, but Asher knew better. The Navy had nothing to do with his father being an absent dad.

She embraced his little body and kissed him on the head. "Today, you have gym. It's going to be a good day."

But Asher didn't move. "Please don't make me go."

That's when the tears became a full-out cry. Just like all the other mornings, Stephanie was at a complete loss as to what to do. She cringed as her father's footsteps came down the hall.

"Asher, come on, get up." She pulled back the covers, but Asher grabbed them, pulling them back over him, crying harder.

His door opened, and her dad walked in. "Stop that now, Ash."

"Dad," Stephanie groaned. "Let me handle my son."

"He needs to get up and ready for school. That's life, and he needs to get used to it, not be coddled," her father said.

Asher stifled his crying at this point, but out of fear, not comfort.

"Go to school or pull up pots in the cold rain with Pops." Her father furrowed his hairy gray eyebrows at Asher.

Asher snuck a look at Stephanie, but he knew better than to think she had any control over her father. The "you're living under my roof" discussions had begun well before Asher could talk.

Stephanie loved her father and knew he'd move heaven and earth for his daughters, but his lack of empathy and restraint grated on her.

Another reason she wanted the position at the Abbott house was that she could maybe earn enough to save and move out. She loved her father, but she wanted to keep a loving relationship with him. But right now, what she wanted to say to him wouldn't be very loving.

She kissed Asher on the forehead, wiping away the lingering tears. "Go wash up before the bus comes."

She reached over to the nightstand and turned off the light. She didn't like Asher having to take the bus, but asking her dad never worked.

Asher dragged himself out of bed, put his lovies into his nightstand drawer, and headed to the bathroom before closing the door behind him.

Stephanie walked out to the kitchen. "You know he's just navigating the feeling of abandonment."

"He has a whole family who loves and cares for him. That's all he needs," her father said.

"Asher misses his father," she said.

"Who's an imbecile," her father replied, grabbing his mug and sitting at the table.

Usually, by this time in the morning, if it weren't the winter season, her father would be out on his lobster boat named, *My Girl Sue*, dragging lobster pots out of the Atlantic Ocean. However, the winter months slowed them down.

"Do you need an extra hand fixing any of the cages?" she asked. As a kid, her father would give her twenty bucks a pop for each pot she fixed. With Christmas around the corner, she could use the money. "I could even go out on the boat."

"Are you in trouble?" her father asked, looking concerned. "Since when do you want to fish?"

"Since I became Santa Claus," she hissed in a low voice. She checked over her shoulder to make sure Asher wasn't behind her.

Her father shook his head. "You don't think Gabe's going to get him anything?"

She shook her head. "He'll get him something, but not from Santa."

This made her father grunt some expletives as he opened up the screen to his tablet.

"Isn't that nice of him," he said sarcastically. "He'll probably use the money he owes you in child support."

Not probably, but most definitely. Stephanie didn't want to get into it with her dad. She didn't want to talk about how she'd be the one who looked like she didn't get Asher anything for Christmas, making all the gifts come from Santa Claus under the tree. Meanwhile, Gabe will sweep in when he chooses, loading Asher with presents *from Dad*. Or at least that's what had happened for the past two years Gabe had lived in Portland.

After she'd divorced him, he stopped helping with parenting. He got to be the fun playdate when he felt like having his son come and visit. He only had Asher come down to Portland when it was convenient for him. It didn't matter if Stephanie had work or plans. When Gabe decided he wanted to be with Asher, that's when it had to happen.

As angry and annoyed as she had become with Gabe, she swallowed it all for Asher because he loved his father. When Gabe decided to be a father, he was great at it. He had just been a really bad husband.

"I have some pots that need fixing if you're looking for extra money," her father said, walking back to the kitchen.

She hadn't told him about the interview, but it was Blueberry Bay. Anyone could know her personal life by now. "It's more about being full-time, with health insurance and paid sick leave."

She had better talk to Lindy, her current boss, before finding out.

How sad that Stephanie had dreamed of becoming a doctor or a lawyer, and now she dreamed of retirement plans and 401(k)s.

"Why would you want to work for a family like that?" he said, surprising her.

"I thought you always liked Julian when he came over," she said.

"When he was a kid, but he's not coming over like he did anymore, now is he?" Brian LaBelle looked around his kitchen as if to make a point. "I wonder if he even talks to Will. He's probably just like his parents, who I never liked."

Stephanie had no clue what Julian was like, but she'd be fine dealing with imbeciles if that meant she got health insurance.

"It's a good job," she said.

Her father made a face like he had eaten something sour. "It's your life."

"Let me go out on the boat," she said. "I need more pay and better hours than the diner."

She knew he wouldn't allow her. To Brian LaBelle, the boat was too dangerous for his daughter, and after twenty-six years, she should know better than to ask. Since the day she could walk, Stephanie had wanted to get out on the boat and be just like her father. And her father had done everything to discourage her and bait her brother into the family business.

He would say there wasn't any genderism in his family. He took her out on the boat plenty, but the idea of his daughter fishing, out on the water by herself even... He'd never imagine it, let alone allow her.

She'd have to buy her own boat, which she couldn't afford. She'd have to find someone willing to sponsor her as a sternman for at least two years, which would never happen on the waters around Blueberry Bay. The code among lobstermen was iron-clad. No one would betray Brian LaBelle, especially regarding his daughter. Gabe still didn't go into the house after the first time they split up. Not after his girlfriend had spilled the beans at her father's favorite drinking hole.

She didn't need another thing for her father to be right about. Her father had been right about everything when it came to

Gabe. That he only cared about himself or that he was going to hurt her or that he had been unfaithful. The worst part was she had believed Gabe and not her father or the other woman, even though he'd fooled around right under her nose. It wasn't until the accident, and well, he couldn't hide the girlfriend when his forehead had gone through the windshield of her car.

Stephanie had thought getting pregnant out of wedlock had been the biggest story she'd be a part of in Blueberry Bay. But the gossip of her husband's affair had spread like wildfire. It had even hit the newspaper because the state had charged his girlfriend with a felony DUI with injury, and Gabe had felt bad for *her*.

The only positive aspect of it all was that Asher was too young to remember any of it. Stephanie had truly missed her calling, which could've been acting. With the way she played along with Asher as if his father is a hero in the Navy, not a devil in uniform, she could win an Academy Award.

"What's wrong?" Will asked as soon as he walked down the back staircase to the kitchen. Her older brother wasn't genuinely asking; more like checking the room's temperature. He must've heard something before coming downstairs.

"Your sister wants to work for the Abbotts." Brian LaBelle turned his back to both his children as he muttered, "Who'd ever want to work for those sons of b—"

"Pops, really?" she said as Asher's footsteps pounded down the hallway.

She missed her mom so much.

After a small tug-of-war, Asher got on the bus since Miss Linda, the bus driver, had offered the seat up front next to her. Another concern for Stephanie was that she needed to follow up with Mrs. Merrill. Asher didn't seem to be finding many friends, if any at all. He had his neighborhood friends and the playdates she set up, but no school friends ever asked him to play or invited him over.

Thoughts rambled around as she headed off to work. She walked instead of driving. The December morning had a bit of humidity, which softened the bite of the cold temperatures, even though the thermometer registered at ten degrees Fahrenheit. She'd layer up. Anything could do to save a few bucks.

Her family home sat on the hilltop of Blueberry Bay, overlooking the small New England town. Behind the white Congregational church, the small fisherman's cape had a wraparound porch and a red barn attached. Growing up, it had been a little girl's dream. A secret passage to the barn through her bedroom closet. A rope swing hanging in the barn. A creek meandering through the backyard. The Atlantic Ocean was a bike ride away.

She walked past the fire station and onto Ocean Avenue, where most restaurants and shops were located, including Lindy's Diner. All the storefronts had already been decorated for Christmas. She stopped in front of the flower shop, which used seashells and sand dollars in the garland, and a starfish on the top of a beautifully decorated Christmas tree. She had almost forgot about the shell tradition for the town Christmas tree.

She imagined what she'd do if she could decorate the inside of the Abbott house with their kind of money. She'd hire the local florist, Nancy, who'd grown up with her mother, and fill the house with floor-to-ceiling garland, lights, and ornaments. She'd drape it all along the fence and along every mantel and tabletop and shelf in each room. Using tasteful decorations, she'd incorporate art and whimsical antiques. She'd have a twenty-foot-plus balsam fir displayed in white lights, and a children's-themed tree in the lounge off the hallway with bright-colored bulbs. It would be a winter wonderland full of Christmas magic.

Since her father happened to fall on the Grinch side of the Christmas spectrum, she didn't get carried away with decorating. She'd get away with most of the stuff she placed around the house with the excuse it had been her mother's old things, but one day, she promised, as she looked inside the window, she'd decorate her *own* place just as beautifully.

Off in the distance, the school bell rang out. She was almost late for her shift. She hurried the rest of the way, speeding past the bookstore—her next favorite stop—and walked-jogged the rest of the way to Lindy's Diner.

Even though the morning rush had technically died down, at nine o'clock the place was buzzing, filled with the local regulars and a few out-of-towners. Usually, she made a decent amount if she could get the morning or dinner rush, but the lunch shift worked better for her schedule. She'd get home just in time for dinner and could do bedtime with Asher.

Lindy looked up from the counter as she walked through the door and lifted her eyebrow.

*She knows,* Stephanie said in her head.

"You have a visitor," Lindy said, nodding toward the booths.

Julian Abbott was at the very end, with his back facing her.

"How long has he been here?" she asked. He'd just called her that morning.

"Long enough to ask when you're getting here twice." Lindy winked at her. "You better hurry over there. You should never keep a handsome man waiting."

Stephanie shook her head. "Oh, no, nothing is going on between the two of us."

"I know," Lindy said, as though her wink was for something else.

"I meant to tell you that—"

"You applied for Janet's job." Lindy stuffed a menu back into its slot.

"I guess you do know." Stephanie grabbed an apron and looked at Julian sitting in her section, who still hadn't turned around. She walked over with a pitcher of ice water and a glass. She poured before he even noticed she was standing there.

"Stephanie," he said, looking up. "I didn't see you come in."

"Hard to see when your back is facing the front," she said, gesturing the pitcher toward the entrance. "What can I get you?"

"I'm here to apologize for what I said." Julian frowned. "I shouldn't have suggested waiting tables was a lower job than being a housekeeper."

So that's what a house manager was—a housekeeper. "Well, thank you for the apology."

She looked back at the front. A group of four women walked in. They'd easily be a hundred-dollar table and a great tip. But Julian took up the booth.

"Are you planning on staying?" she asked, hoping he'd leave.

He looked over to the side of the table, where he slid the menu in front of him. "I guess I'll need a minute."

She silently groaned as Lindy took the group to another section. "Great. Let me know when you're ready."

She whipped back to the counter to take care of some single diners. Her real bread and butter were the old men of Blueberry Bay.

"How's it going, Dr. Gordon?" she asked one of her favorite regulars.

"Can't complain. You?" he asked as she filled his mug of coffee.

"Never better." She set the creamer next to him. "Are you going to stick with an omelet this morning?"

Gordon Johnson hadn't practiced medicine for over a decade, but he'd stepped right in and performed CPR when a customer had a heart attack during one of Stephanie's shifts. He'd saved Rick Sylvester's life that morning, and the whole town of Blueberry Bay had called him Dr. Gordon from that point on.

"I think I will," he said, handing the menu he knew by heart over to her.

"I'll be back with your orange juice," she said, sliding the *Boston Globe* across the counter to him.

"Sounds great," he said, looking over his shoulder toward Julian. "Ah, look who it is."

He stood up, left his seat, and walked over to Julian. Stephanie watched as the older man hugged Julian and then sat down across from him. Just as she wondered how the two knew each other so well, she realized the connection between the families. Julian's brother, Oliver, was married to Dr. Gordon's granddaughter, Cora. The small town of Blueberry Bay was getting even smaller.

She returned to Julian's table with a coffee mug and set it down. "Would you like to move to this table?"

Dr. Gordon smiled at this and looked across to Julian. "That's a great idea."

But she saw Julian grimace. Maybe her father was right. Perhaps it was best she hadn't gotten the job.

Julian ended up sticking with a cup of coffee, wasting a perfectly large booth that could seat up to six, to him and Dr. Gordon with one omelet and an orange juice. With the morning crowd dwindling, Stephanie decided to do her side work—filling the salt and pepper shakers, adding ketchup and mustard to their containers, and wiping down all the menus.

As customers came and went, Dr. Gordon and Julian sat in her booth, drinking free refills and talking. They had been so wrapped up in their conversation that they hadn't even noticed when she stood at their table with their check.

"I should get going," Julian said. "Good to see you."

He dropped a pile of twenties on the table, too much for the cup of coffee, and slid out of the booth.

"It's on me," he said to Dr. Gordon.

"Good man," Dr. Gordon said as he tucked his wallet into his pocket.

"That's way too much," Stephanie said, picking up the twenties.

Julian shrugged. "We took up your time and the table."

She held out the money to him. "Yes, but this is over a hundred dollars."

Julian waved at it. "Merry Christmas."

As she stretched out the twenties, Julian walked away, leaving the booth and diner before she could protest.

Dr. Gordon pulled himself out of the booth and donned his winter coat. Stephanie grabbed hold of his collar and helped him put it on.

"Julian mentioned you were thinking of working as his family's house manager," Dr. Gordon said.

So Julian was just like the locals. Gossipy. "Yes, I applied."

"Good family," Dr. Gordon said.

She almost wanted to tell him what her father had said about Julian but changed her mind. "I don't know them."

"Really?" Dr. Gordon's forehead wrinkled. "Julian said you two used to play as kids."

Quickly, she glanced out the window to see Julian enter a black sedan that shined, even parked in a snowy puddle. He stared back into the restaurant through his windshield. She narrowed her eyes back at him. She'd give his pity money back. She didn't need another person gossiping about her. Did she come off as desperate? She looked down at her outfit. Her pair of jeans were definitely outdated, but in decent condition. Her sneakers had seen better days, but why get new ones when she's had so many people spill something on her?

As Julian pulled out of his parking space, she looked down at the money in her hand, annoyed he didn't listen to her and take it back. He thought he was doing her a favor, but it only solidified her decision to turn down his stupid trial period offer. Her dad was right again. She didn't want to work for people like Julian Abbott. She dropped the dirty dishes back on the table and ran out of the diner after him.

And she didn't want his money.

# CHAPTER 4

*W*hen Julian met his eyes with Stephanie's, he assumed she was grateful for the thoughtful tip. A truce of sorts. When their stare broke, he went back to reversing his car. So, when she stormed out of the diner, shaking the money in her hand, he almost didn't see her and slammed on his brakes, which made her stop short and stumble off the sidewalk, and her foot splashed into a puddle of slush.

Her eyes widened as the cold must have hit her. He immediately turned off the car and got out.

"Here." She shoved the money at him. "I don't need anything more than what you owe."

What had he done that had offended her so badly? It was normal to get a trial period in most jobs. He understood she had a family to consider, but it wasn't like she couldn't get a job waiting tables elsewhere.

She huffed as she turned back to the diner.

And that's when he heard himself.

"I'm a jerk. It's why I don't go places."

She stopped and faced him. Her eyebrows lifted. If she hadn't thought he was loony before, she definitely thought he was losing it now.

"Seriously, I'm sorry," he said, unable to stop talking and putting his foot in his mouth. He shrugged, stuffing the money into his back pocket. "I—just—should—"

He held his hands up as if surrendering, stepping back toward his car. He had no idea why his mouth kept moving and words kept pouring out, but he needed them to stop, considering the look she gave him made him feel even crazier.

"You're not a jerk," she said before he got into the car. "At least from what I remember."

He looked up at her. Did she remember hanging out with him? He wasn't sure. The other day at the house, she'd acted as though they had been strangers.

"I should go back in." She crossed her arms, the cold getting to her. "Thanks for the generous tip, but it's just not necessary."

He gave her a nod, feeling foolish and completely Abbott, stuffing his money in people's faces to fix his problems. She turned to walk back into the diner when he shouted out.

"Wait!" He knew his grandfather would adore her. He'd get over Julian pulling his weight over Janet since the two-week trial was her idea. "You don't need the trial. You can have the job."

She didn't move or say anything.

"I mean, if you still want it."

He'd pay a huge price for this. Janet loved holding grudges. It was obvious from that morning sitting in the diner that Stephanie was a hard worker. She was good with the customers, quick and efficient, and smart-witted. She could carry a conversation with everyone, even people she didn't particularly seem to enjoy, like himself.

"You're not hiring Janet's niece?"

He shook his head.

"Do you have a minute?" he asked, looking back at the restaurant.

"Not really," she said, rubbing her arms as her body shivered.

He didn't know how to move forward. "Give me a call if you're interested."

He almost pulled out his card, but didn't want to appear more pompous than he already had and instead pulled out the receipt he had stuffed in his pocket. He grabbed a pen from inside his car before quickly jotting down his number. "Here."

He passed the paper to her. At one time, he'd hand her his flashy black card with his information and a highly coveted title. Now, he wrote a number on a crinkled receipt.

She took her fingers and straightened the receipt, then folded it carefully in half. "Nice to see you again, Julian."

And with that, she took off inside the diner, back behind the counter. As he got into his car, he saw her talking to customers through the window. Right back to doing her job. Completely professional.

When he arrived at his grandfather's, he went straight to Janet to confess what he had done.

"You hired her without a trial period?" Janet folded her hands together, a sign she was agitated. "Without consulting me?"

"I'll help train her," he said.

She walked over to her office, a small room off the kitchen. She picked up a four-inch binder, then another and another, dumping each heavy, paper-filled organizer in his arms.

"What's all this?" he asked.

"Her training." Janet looked amused. "Your grandmother had precise instructions on caring for this house."

Labeled with different topics—cleaning and caretaking, house calendar, house maintenance—it started to sink in how little Julian actually knew about Janet's job.

"Your family has dozens of priceless pieces of art and furniture." Janet pointed to the binder in the middle. "They're all surviving the Atlantic Ocean's salty air because I have meticulously taken care of things around here like your grandmother wanted."

Julian set the heavy binders down on top of Janet's desk. "You've done a great job."

Janet nodded. "I think you're thinking with your heart and not your head on this one."

"I want someone I can trust." And something about Stephanie, even if he hadn't spent time with her in over a decade, made him believe he could trust her.

Janet walked back toward her desk and sat down. She didn't say anything for what felt like forever. Julian imagined having to tell Stephanie that he messed up again. Then finally, Janet said, "She can start Monday."

She started clicking the keys to her computer, her attention on something else, and ignoring Julian's presence at this point.

"Well, she hasn't exactly accepted the job," he said, wincing as Janet slowly turned back to face him.

"She didn't take your offer?" Janet's eyes flashed with bewilderment. "What is it about this girl?"

"Nothing," he said, but he didn't understand it himself. "I always really enjoyed the LaBelles growing up. Having someone I know and feel comfortable around would be nice. Like you." Janet felt more like family than someone who worked for them. "It's going to be weird having someone here that doesn't know us."

Janet gave him a small smile at that one. "But it's not about you. It's about your grandfather."

"He's going to love her." But he wasn't exactly sure. He was only going on what he remembered from when he was a kid. She had just chewed him out for offering her the job that she applied for. Maybe the sweet Stephanie changed when that loser Gabe left the picture. "I mean, I think he'll like her."

Janet gave him that look she did when she thought he was being an idiot. She sighed, exaggerating the long and heavy breath before saying, "If she doesn't work out, that will be on you." She pulled out the binder with *Cleaning and Caretaking* titled on it. "Your grandmother called it the first and most important pillar of them all."

Julian took the binder and headed to the television room to

study the first pillar of being a house manager. As he opened the cover, he couldn't believe his eyes when he saw his grandmother's writing on the first page.

*To Whom It May Concern:*

*This is an old house, with old furniture and old memories, but that also inspires new beginnings and new memories and new dreams. Do take special care of the things that encourage play and imagination.*

A wave of grief washed over him as he stared at his grandmother's writing. Always the maternal figure in his life, Julian had been hit hard when she'd died of a heart attack. A hole in his heart had been left with her passing. Like a beacon of light, she had been the one who'd brought the family together. They hadn't gotten together as an entire family since her passing. Not even on her favorite holiday, Christmas.

He flipped through the binder's pages to the holiday section. Every ornament, Christmas decoration, and package of lights were listed in order and with a location and placement map. Everything had been typed by what looked like an old computer with large pixels. Most of the printed text had faded to a faint gray. But in every margin, in ink, was his grandmother's handwriting. *Santa sleigh by the kids' bedrooms*, she'd written next to the item that was listed as St. Nick's Toboggan.

Julian flipped through the pages and thought back to the memories of the time in his life he'd felt the magic of Christmas. Being a child in his grandparents' home had been like living in a real-life fairy tale—toys and games and the beach. He closed the cover, looking around the room that hadn't been decorated for Christmas since his grandmother had died.

"How's it going?" Janet asked, walking into the room. She carried a tray of tea and a small plate of snacks. She usually didn't cater to Julian, never serving him like this.

"Good," he said, watching Janet settle into the small couch across the room.

"I think it's time we talk about some things, before she accepts the job," Janet said.

"What things?" Julian didn't understand.

Janet sighed. "You have no idea about the vultures that swarm."

"Vultures?"

"Your family, cousins, aunts, uncles—they all want to get their hands on things in that binder." Janet pointed to the book. "But it's only your grandfather's."

"Are you suggesting that people are stealing from my grandfather?" Julian didn't think his family would stoop that low.

"No, but maybe borrow his first edition of Janet Eyre for a girlfriend…" Janet gave him a pointed look.

He had forgotten he had taken the classic for a girl he'd had a thing for at Cornell.

"I guess I can see your point." He looked at the binder. "Where is all of this stuff anyway?"

"The basement mostly." Janet looked down at the page. "Ah, the Christmas stuff is in the guest house."

Julian wondered if it would be worth dragging things like that out. Would his grandfather even want it out? "When was the last time we decorated?"

But he knew the answer. Since his grandmother died. But Janet didn't answer anyway; just dropped her head to one side and raised her eyebrows the way she did when she was judging him.

"Well, now that Oliver is married, maybe you should bring back some traditions," she said.

Julian shrugged. He didn't know why, but decorating and celebrating the holiday like old times seemed very appealing.

Janet thought about it for a moment. "I'll tell you what. Why don't you make it the new-girl's project."

The idea of having to celebrate the holiday with his folks without having a drink seemed too much at this point in his sobriety. "I think we should have her focus on the day-to-day things before decorating."

And as if the universe had heard Janet, Julian's phone rang with an unfamiliar number.

"Hello?" he said, answering it.

"Julian, it's Stephanie LaBelle."

He covered the phone's mouthpiece. "It's her."

Janet rolled her eyes, but she waited to hear.

"I decided to accept your offer for the job," Stephanie said.

Did he hear hesitation in her voice?

"That's great," he said. "You can start Monday."

"I have to give my current place of work a two-week notice," she said.

He hadn't thought about her current work. Did the diner really need two weeks to find and train a replacement? He shook his head at his own ridiculousness. Yes, of course they did. He thought about a saying Brandon used frequently. *Let go. Move on.*

*Shift the conversation*, he thought to himself.

"We're happy to hear you're joining our household."

He looked at Janet to see if that sounded creepy, but she didn't react.

"I look forward to getting to know you all," she said. Then threw out, "Again."

"Yeah, totally," he said, feeling awkward suddenly.

"Julian?" she said.

"Yeah?" He waited for her to change her mind.

"Thanks for taking a chance on me."

And he let out a sigh of relief.

"Like I said, we look forward to working with you." He tried to sound as professional as possible. He didn't want Janet to think he had anything other than professional feelings for Stephanie. "If you need to give your current employer two weeks"—Janet's eyes bulged— "then we'll have to wait two weeks."

"I'll try and swing in as much as I can in the meantime," Stephanie said. "I just have to find care for my son."

"Bring him here," Julian offered, turning his back to Janet. He already knew she was going to flip out about the two weeks.

"Bring him here?!" Janet hissed out in a whisper, but he was almost certain Stephanie could hear her.

"Seriously?" Stephanie asked. "You don't mind having a six-year-old around?"

"Is he potty trained?" Julian said it to be funny, but Stephanie answered seriously.

"Yes, he is."

He couldn't read her tone, which had been his specialty up to that point. Julian never had any trouble reading people. When he had been drinking, he'd get personal fast, dipping into people, asking questions about them, and they'd reveal everything in return. Julian wasn't the kind of drunk that got upset, quite the opposite. He was so pleasant and fun to be around, people would count on his promises. But when he became sober and returned to the honest Julian, he'd forget all about the promises.

Because the real Julian, the sober one, wasn't all that nice of a person. And the drunk one was a fake.

When Julian drank, people around him felt more at ease than with the ridged sober Julian. His brother proved that theory every time they tried to go out. They had less and less to talk about these days. That's why he was such a good salesman for the commercial loan department at the company. He could schmooze the hardest hardball into the best-bud zone. By the time Julian had them making a deal and giving him a handshake, he also had their wives in his pocket. But then came the next day, and Julian would forget what he had promised to whom and how low the interest rate was.

It hadn't caught up to him at work, all the little white lies he'd said to land a deal while boozing with clients. He'd lie about the littlest things, like how he loved to play golf, tennis, or pickleball; it didn't matter. It would be his favorite if it was the other person's favorite. He was so phony during his six years working for Diversified Business and Credit that he'd almost forgotten what he actually did and didn't like.

Janet stood staring at him as he hung up.

"What did you do?" she asked, putting her hands on her hips.

"I offered her the job," he said, looking down at his phone to avoid Janet's eyes.

"But we're not a daycare." Janet furrowed her eyebrows.

"You brought Billy Jr. around," Julian said about Janet's son who he had to play with as a kid. He couldn't stand the pudgy know-it-all.

"To keep you out of your mother's hair." Janet wasn't holding back, apparently. "What is it with this girl?"

"She's a mother who needs to bring her son if she's going to come in before she officially starts." He needed to stick with the facts, because he wasn't sure why he was bending over backward for her. "I don't know. I feel sorry for her, I guess."

"Stephanie doesn't need anyone to feel sorry for her," Janet said. "She got herself into that mess all on her own." Janet walked to the kitchen sink and turned on the faucet.

Julian had to stop and think for a minute. Was she referring to Stephanie's son as the mess? "What mess?"

"She and Gabe had Asher when they were kids." Janet shut off the water and wiped her hands with a towel. "She happened to get pregnant right when Gabe was leaving for deployment. She knew what kind of man Gabe was by then."

The innuendo made his stomach turn. The young woman he remembered had more going for her than having Gabe Turner as a husband. "I feel like it might've been the other way around."

Janet's eyebrows raised.

Julian shrugged. He shouldn't even say anything. "I mean, she had everything going for her before Gabe got her pregnant."

"Right..." Janet put her hands on her hips while shaking her head. "Well, good luck, because I'm leaving after the new year. Now that she's starting two weeks later, she'll only have a few days with me."

"A few days?"

"I'm taking my Christmas vacation." Janet's face twisted.

"Oh, right, Christmas."

"Maybe you could at least put up a tree for your brother and his new wife," Janet suggested.

Julian shook his head. "Nah, I don't think that's a good idea."

"You, of all people, understand the importance of moving on and letting go." Janet tilted her head at him like she always did to make sure he was paying attention to what she was saying.

"I don't think losing the ability to drink is the same as losing your wife of fifty years." Julian knew he was using his grandfather's grief as an excuse, because it was really him who didn't want the decorations up.

"All I'm saying is that your grandfather should be making more memories with his family and remembering the good times," she said. "Do you think your grandmother wanted all those Christmas decorations to sit in a barn? She spent years collecting all the individual ornaments and decorations, planning and prepping. It's a shame you all let that go."

Julian wasn't the one who loved Christmas, but as he stood there with gingerbread dancing in his head, he had to admit his grandmother had made Christmas magical. Traveling all the way up to the coast of Maine and celebrating Christmas together as one big happy family had been some of the best moments of his life.

He looked around the space. "No, we aren't decorating."

# CHAPTER 5

"*I*'m sorry, but I can't watch Asher tonight," Will said as he picked up the keys to his truck. "I've got a date."

"Really, who?" Stephanie couldn't believe him.

"With a girl named Margarita." Will thought the whole quip made him look clever, but it made Stephanie's blood boil.

"Can't you skip going to the bars for one night?" She didn't want to take Asher the first night she went to the Abbott house.

"I worked all day," he said. "I get to spend some time out with my friends. It's Thursday night trivia. Where are you going?"

She shook her head. She couldn't believe her brother. She rarely asked him to help with Asher, and he wouldn't even consider changing his plans to help her out just this once—plans he had every Thursday and Friday and Saturday night.

"I need to go to the Abbotts. Remember my new job?" she reminded him. "You'll see all the guys tomorrow night, too."

"Why are you working for them anyway?" Will said it like he was eating something rotten.

"Because I want health insurance." Why was that so hard for her family to understand?

He rolled his eyes. "If you want to work for pompous snobs, be my guest."

She clenched her fists, wishing she could go back to being a kid again and whack him. Her brother didn't see how different his life was compared to hers. Her father had no problem helping his son get his fishing license and sponsoring him to become a sternman. Her father even helped him with a down payment for a commercial-size lobster boat. She swallowed her annoyance and walked away. It was her fault she had forgotten that her father had his bowling league tonight when she'd offered to go to the Abbotts. Usually, her dad would take Asher, which really meant Asher was on his own while her father watched television.

She hoped Julian had been serious when he said she could bring her kid, because she was about to bring her kid.

"Get your book and coloring stuff," she said as she entered his room. She grabbed his backpack, which she had filled with activities he could do at the diner when she needed to take him there.

She knew Asher would be a good boy and wouldn't cause trouble. But she had learned that people had opinions of women taking their children to the workplace, as if it were negligent. No one ever asked where Gabe was or why he never took his son to help out. Or ask why he didn't offer to pay for daycare or child support. Instead, people would make comments about her working and her child sitting in a diner. One time she'd given him her phone, and almost everyone at the diner had had an opinion about it.

"Why?" Asher looked up from the action figures he was playing with.

"Because Mommy has to work tonight," she said. She waited for the meltdown.

"But I don't want to go to the diner."

"You're not going to the diner," she said, grabbing hold of his hand and dragging him to the window. She pointed out. Even though it was technically still afternoon, the sky was as black as night. "We're going to the big house across the bay."

Asher dropped his figures on the sill and pressed his face

against the window, holding his hands around his eyes to see out. "Really? Why?"

"Because Mommy got a new job," she said, feeling a bit proud. "I'm going to help them care for that beautiful house."

Asher kept his face against the window and said, "Why?"

He was killing her with the whys. "Because they need help. It's so big."

"Wow," he said. "Can I bring my Transformers?"

She didn't know what the Abbotts' opinions would be about her parenting, but she was sure about one thing: they'd have one.

"Sure."

When she got everything together, she got a reluctant Asher into the car and drove to the Abbotts' house.

When they arrived at the gate, the doors that had been closed before were now left open.

"This is their house?" Asher asked from the back seat.

She didn't pull into the driveway initially; she just stared down the long drive to the massive white house anchored at the end. She finally pulled forward, slowly moving up the drive. "It sure is."

All her inferiority came out in her sweaty palms as she slid the car into park. She wiped them on her black pants and took a deep breath before opening her door.

"Okay, here we go," Stephanie said in her most chipper voice.

"Can I eat my nighttime snacks?" he asked, leaving the car.

"Yes, if you ask for permission." She held out her hand, waiting for Asher to take it, and they walked up to the house together.

What was she doing taking this job? And bringing her child! This house and the people inside were way out of her league. She had cleaned for the bumbling men in her life, but they were far from Abbotts.

She'd done all she could to research Maxwell Abbott. He had been CEO and chair of the largest investment firm in New England and, at one time, the United States. He had buildings and schools and scholarships all named after him. He had news stories written about him. He had graced several magazines and dated a movie star before meeting the love of his life.

Max had married his wife, Corrine, in a small ceremony on the Cape, with only family and friends in attendance. They had three children, but Steven, their oldest son, was the only Abbott child to go into the family business. It looked to Stephanie that once Steven took a more public role at his father's investment firm, Max Abbott had felt safe to venture into politics, becoming a US Senator. Now retired, he'd lost his beloved wife five years ago and lived with his grandson Julian at his Maine mega-mansion.

There was no way she would be able to do this.

The house and grounds had been illuminated by lights, the white exterior bright against the inky black sky. She looked across the bay to see if she could find her own house, but there were no lights pointing it out.

A harsh wind blew as they reached the side door, and just like Janet had instructed, she knocked instead of ringing the doorbell.

Janet opened the door almost immediately, as though she had been waiting for them to arrive.

"Good evening," she said to Stephanie, and then she looked down at Asher. "Good to see you, Asher."

Asher looked up at the unfamiliar face and leaned in closer to Stephanie. "Hi."

"He'll be no trouble," Stephanie said, putting her arm around him. "He's got plenty to keep him busy while I'm here."

Janet nodded. "Good. Well, then. Let's begin." Janet pointed to the kitchen table and said to Asher, "You can set up your stuff here."

Asher walked over to the long wooden table and dropped his book bag on top. He then pulled out some of the snacks he had packed.

"Asher," Stephanie said, hoping that would remind him to ask.

Asher looked up and said, "May I eat my snacks?"

"Yes, you may, but you need to clean up after yourself," Janet said.

Stephanie smiled at Asher as he opened up his snack pack. He then pulled out all his action figures and crowded them together in a pile next to his food.

"Be careful not to scratch the table with those." Janet sounded like a teacher.

"I will," Asher said, dangling his feet as he bit into a slice of apple.

"Let's begin in the kitchen," Janet said, walking down a short hall to a doorway. "This will be your office."

Stephanie looked into the small room with no exterior windows. It had a desk and a few shelves. A vacuum stood in the corner, next to a lamp and a chair. Two paintings and a calendar hung on the wall. It wasn't much, but Stephanie had never had an office before.

"This will be my office?" She couldn't believe it.

Janet looked like she couldn't believe it either. "Yes."

The older woman sat down behind the desk. She pushed three black binders filled with papers toward Stephanie.

"These will be your lifeline for the next however many years you work here," Janet said.

Stephanie pulled them toward her. "Do you have them digitalized?"

Janet shook her head.

It seemed to her that having at least one digital copy would be a good idea, considering their importance. She opened the cover to see handwriting so neat and perfect. She brushed her fingertips over the indentations from the pen.

"I haven't had the time to do it." Janet exhaled heavily as though it were a silly question.

"I can do that for you," Stephanie said, thinking she could do it after she put Asher down at night.

"Don't you mean for you?" Janet asked. Her eyebrows raised at Stephanie like she was an idiot.

"Yes, I guess you're right." Stephanie stared at the binder.

"You'll want to take these home and learn them." Janet passed another folder with packets of paper to Stephanie. "These are the weekly lists, daily calendars, and other odds and ends that happened this past year. Knowing I was retiring, I made sure to record everything that needed to be done throughout the year."

One thing Janet had going for her was her organization. Everything had been written down and explained in thorough detail. Brand names of products, companies she used, people she hired—everything was listed in an easy-to-find manner. Janet was a girl after her own heart.

"This is wonderful," Stephanie said, closing the folder. "I look forward to digging into this."

Janet huffed at that. "Look, Stephanie, you're a smart girl, but don't get too invested."

"What?" Stephanie felt her stomach sink. "Why?"

"Well, Mr. Abbott is getting older." Janet looked down at her desk, shuffling an already neat pile. "I don't think the family intends to keep the house after he passes."

Stephanie hadn't considered the possibility of the senior Abbott not living across the bay. "Oh."

"Not that it's going to happen anytime soon, but I just want to be upfront with you because I know that boy certainly wasn't."

"That boy?" Stephanie thought she was referring to Asher.

"Julian." Janet sighed. "I love the young man, but he doesn't understand what losing a job means for people who rely on a paycheck."

Stephanie thought about this for a moment. She very much relied on a paycheck, but she also couldn't earn the money or the benefits she needed just by waiting tables. She could always go back to doing that if she needed to.

"I'll just have to follow the strict diet plan listed here," Stephanie said.

Janet gave her a half smile. "There's something you should know about Julian."

Stephanie waited for a bomb to drop. "What is it?"

"He's recently become sober," she said, clasping her hands together. "He's come a long way, but he's fragile. There can't be any alcohol around whatsoever."

"Of course," Stephanie said, wishing Janet hadn't made it some deep, dark secret. "I think that's great."

She did. How many people needed to do just that? Gabe and her marriage might have worked without his constant need for alcohol and going out to the bars. Without alcohol, her brother might actually act like an uncle and hang out with his nephew.

Suddenly, a deep voice could be heard in the kitchen, followed by Asher's.

*Oh no,* Stephanie thought. *Please tell me he's not making a mess with his snacks.*

Janet stopped talking and froze, listening to what was happening in the kitchen. "That would be Julian."

"Should I move Asher?" Stephanie said, getting up to move him right then.

"No, no, they'll be fine," Janet said, shaking her head and going back to the binders. "Let's talk about your typical day."

# CHAPTER 6

*J*ulian was rarely around children. He wasn't exactly sure if he liked them. At least other people's. He hoped that if he were to have his own, he'd like them. He wasn't entirely sure if his father liked him. His father tolerated him at best. His mother loved her children but had been distant at times. Once, he had overheard her complaining to a friend that she regretted losing her ballet career to having children.

"How's it going?" he asked the small boy sitting at the table.

A shiny blue-and-red Transformers backpack sat on the kitchen table. Dozens of Transformer figures splayed out from its opening.

The boy looked up from a snack cup of chocolate pudding and looked petrified. With a full mouth, he asked, "Want some?"

"No thanks, little man," Julian said, as he ripped a paper towel off its roll and passed it over to the chocolate-mustached boy. "Do you have Bumblebee?"

Julian had played with Transformers when he was this kid's age. He had a tiny plastic snack container with pretzels and what he guessed was Nutella. As a kid, Julian had always wanted a packed snack like that. But in the schools he had attended, the schools had provided the snacks in the dining halls. If he'd wanted to buy those kinds of snacks, he'd have had to get on a bus into town from his prep school, then use his spending money on them.

The little boy shook his head. "I keep him at home."

Julian examined the collection; from what he could see, there were only a few of the less popular characters, some of which were broken and damaged. "Smart. You might lose him."

"I'm not allowed to take them to school," he said as though he was going to ask.

"Do you need anything?" Julian asked, looking at the squished-up juice box.

The boy dangled his feet off the chair, swinging them back and forth. He picked up a Transformer and transformed it back to its original shape. "No, thank you."

That's when Julian remembered the playroom. His grandmother had turned the old attic into a magical playroom for her grandchildren. Every single nook and cranny had been used for childhood imagination. She'd had a full-sized "treehouse" built into the rafters, a set of swings hanging next to a curved slide built into the walls, bookshelves revealing hidden passages, and bunk beds for each of her grandchildren with his or her name painted onto the wood.

Then, a horrible thought crossed his mind. What if it didn't look the same? What if it had gone back to being a place to store everything? He hadn't been up there in years.

"You know, there's a cool playroom here. Do you want to check it out?" he asked the little boy.

He looked up at Julian and then said, "My mom told me I'm not allowed to leave with strangers."

Julian laughed to himself. "That's really smart. Want me to ask your mom if you can go with me?"

The boy nodded.

Julian wanted to go up there for himself as well, to see what his grandmother had kept. "Let me go ask her," he said.

He walked to Janet's office and poked his head in. "Hey, sorry to interrupt, but I wondered if I could take your son to the playroom."

Stephanie turned around. Her hair swung back and fell over her shoulders. She was wearing more makeup than usual, which didn't make her any more beautiful, but a different kind of beautiful. That's the kind of beauty Stephanie LaBelle was. She would look stunning in a garbage bag.

"Oh, that's not necessary. Asher can stay where he is." She waved her hand at him. "I don't want to inconvenience you."

"It's not a problem at all," Julian said. "I think we still have some of my old Transformers."

Janet's eyebrows rose, watching the exchange. "Your grandfather wouldn't let me touch a thing up there."

Julian smiled at that. "Good. Then it should be just perfect for your son."

"Asher," Stephanie said as though he didn't know.

"Asher."

The shock stick hit him. Little Stephanie was a mom and had married one of the biggest jerks in town, Gabe Turner. How had the guy gotten such a sweet and kind person like Stephanie in the first place? Will should have done a better job protecting his little sister.

He gave a little salute and walked away before Janet said something that would embarrass them all.

"Mom says you can play upstairs if you want," he said, thinking the little boy would jump off his chair and run upstairs with the opportunity, but he didn't move.

"I'm okay," he said, his feet swinging back and forth.

"There's cool stuff up there, like the original Transformers," Julian cajoled. "Even a Bumblebee."

The boy shook his head. "No, thanks." He played with the figures.

At this point, the women came out of the office and walked

into the kitchen. Janet seemed to be laughing at something, and both stopped when they saw them.

"I thought you were going up to the attic?" Janet said.

"Umm…" Julian looked at the little boy opening up a Transformer into a car.

He pushed it around the table, not looking at anyone.

"Did you hear there's a swing set up there?" Stephanie said. "I heard there was even a treehouse."

Julian and Asher looked at her. He had forgotten she would have heard about the attic from when her brother Will would come over.

"There is?" Asher's eyes widened.

"And secret passages…" Stephanie walked over to her son. "I promise I'll be right here when you want to see me. I'm not going anywhere."

And it hit Julian. Asher didn't want to leave his mom.

"We don't have to go up there without Mom. We can hang out down here, and I can bring some of the Transformers down to you."

Asher continued to push the toy around the table as he thought. "Can I finish my snack up there?"

"Nope," Stephanie said. "Food is for the kitchen." She stopped and held up her finger as Asher was about to say something. "Unless there's a special event."

Asher looked at the half-transformed broken toy he held in his hand. "Okay."

With a wave of his hand, Julian gave Asher a big smile. "Come follow."

Julian walked toward the front hall and up to the attic, hoping Asher would walk beside him, but Asher lagged behind, following from five feet or more. As they walked, Julian would slow down or come to a complete stop so that Asher could catch up. When they finally reached the top stair, which opened up to the attic, Asher's eyes widened in delight.

"This is an attic?" Asher ran toward the hanging swings.

"Yup," Julian said, stunned himself at the way everything had been kept the same. Why hadn't he come up here? It had one of the best views in the house. The large dormered windows had panoramic views of the ocean. Not to mention the widow's walk that Asher had already started climbing the spiral staircase to get to.

"You can see all of Maine from there," Julian said as Asher reached the top.

"I can see my house!" Asher pointed out toward the bay.

Julian needed to explore and see what was still there. When was the last time he had come up to the attic? Over a decade, at least. The last time he could recall was when he'd brought up some model he had dated from the city. He certainly hadn't played in it.

He walked over to the built-in drawers where the small toys were stored, right where he'd left them. He picked up a plastic box that held his Transformers.

"Here they are." Julian held up the box as Asher came down the stairs.

"You said you have Bumblebee?" Asher asked. He jumped off the bottom step and ran up to the box.

"I even have the original Optimus." Julian pulled apart the Velcro strip to open the cover. Inside, just like he'd left them, lay all of his best Transformers.

"Wow!" Asher said, his hand reaching out to touch, but he stopped. "May I?"

The six-year-old had more manners than most of the men Julian had worked with in banking.

"Of course you may." He nodded his head in the direction of Optimus.

Asher reached right for him and pulled the largest Transformer out of its space.

"He's heavy," Asher said.

"They were made with real metal back when I was a kid. Not

all plastic like nowadays." Julian pulled out his Bumblebee. "What do you think?"

"These are really cool," Asher said, his eyes wide with excitement.

"There's a lot more stuff," Julian said. "The only rule is to return anything you take out."

Asher nodded. "I will."

"You want to set up over here?" Julian pointed to the low table that sat along the built-ins, meant for this exact kind of playing.

Asher took the box right out of Julian's hands and went to where he pointed. With a little chuckle, Julian watched as Asher set up.

"Are you going to play?" Asher asked.

Julian shook his head. He walked over to the other drawers and opened another to see what lay inside. "I don't want to bother you."

Julian hadn't played in decades. Did he even have an imagination any longer?

"It's a lot of fun," Asher said, pulling out more Transformers.

"I have played plenty," Julian said, pulling out his Star Wars figures.

"I hope I don't stop playing." Asher held Optimus up into the air and crashed him onto the table with the others while making noises for each crash. Then he lowered his voice and said, "Bumblebee, let's get the bad guys."

Hesitating for another minute, Julian then pulled out a chair and grabbed Megatron. And with as low of a voice as he could muster, Julian said, "You will never get me, Optimus."

Asher's face lit up as a huge smile grew. He sat up on his knees, getting a higher angle, and moved his figures toward Megatron. "You'll never get away with this, Megatron. We'll stop you."

The two boys played. At first, Julian felt mortified as he deepened his voice for Megatron, but Asher seemed delighted and played even more. Asher made more sounds and added some dialogue, and after saving all the Transformers from Megatron's evils, Bumblebee defeated Megatron with the help of Optimus.

"Good job, Bumblebee," a female voice said from behind.

Julian turned to see Stephanie and Janet standing at the top of the stairs.

Asher dropped the toys and ran right to his mother. "They have every Transformer!"

"Wow," Stephanie said, rubbing Asher's head with her hand. She combed her fingers through his straight blond hair. "We need to get going now."

"Aww, can we stay for a little longer?" Asher asked.

Stephanie shook her head. "No, I'm afraid we've taken enough time from Janet tonight."

"It's fine," Janet said, even though she had originally been upset with Julian for adding extra time to her day to meet Stephanie after her shift at the diner.

"Thank you so much," Stephanie said to Janet. "I'm going to study those binders inside and out."

Stephanie pointed to the table where they had been playing. "Go clean up your mess."

"But I wasn't the only one playing," Asher complained.

"Mr. Abbott will help," Janet said, the left side of her mouth perking up.

Julian did just that. He helped Asher pick up all the rest of the toys and place them back into their box. He then opened the drawer for Asher to put them inside.

"Wow, you have all these Legos?" Asher's attention moved right to the primary-colored assorted bricks.

Oliver's childhood obsession. Oliver had loved building.

"Do you like them?" Julian asked.

"Yes!" Asher's hand went to one of the bins filled with blue bricks.

But before he touched them, Stephanie took hold of it and carefully closed the drawer. "Maybe another time, if Mr. Abbott would let you play again."

"We can come up here the next time you come over," Julian said.

Stephanie was surprised Julian was willing to give Asher the time of day.

"Say thank you to Mr. Abbott, Asher," she said, holding his hand in hers.

Asher shoulders drooped at that. "Thank you, Mr. Abbott."

"My pleasure," he said back. Curiosity was killing him. Why did Stephanie seem so upset?

He followed the group down the stairs and into the main hallway. When they reached the first floor and the door, Asher took his already packed backpack from Stephanie and looked like he was about to put it on his back, but instead, he pulled out an action figure Julian hadn't seen before.

"This is a Quintesson High Commander robot," Asher said seriously, handing Julian the figure.

"Wow, he's high up there," Julian said, not remembering what all that meant, but this only made Asher nod.

"You can have him take watch for the head commander," Asher said in what sounded like an official voice.

It took everything in Julian not to smile. Instead, he took the figure, saluted Asher, and nodded to Stephanie. "I'll take him to his command post right away."

This made Asher happy. He leaned into Stephanie and looked up at her. "Can I come next time?"

Janet made a low grunt, but Julian ignored it. He hoped Stephanie hadn't heard over Asher begging to come back.

"You're always welcome," Julian said, ignoring Janet. He knew this wouldn't be allowed. He was positive that even his kind old grandfather wouldn't want his workers to bring their kids to the job. But how could he tell this sweet boy no?

"That's very nice, Mr. Abbott, but little boys need to go to bed earlier than nine o'clock," Stephanie said, gesturing her head at the large grandfather clock.

He hadn't even noticed the time. Not that he cared much

these days. Either he was sleeping it away or wishing it would go back so he could change things.

"Right, yeah," he said as Janet opened the door for them.

"Children underfoot make things a bit more difficult," Janet said in a very upbeat tone, but she clearly wanted to make a point.

"No, no, it was just for tonight," Stephanie said. "My dad couldn't watch him."

"Any night, seriously," Julian said, using his business voice. "He's always welcome to come and play. Children were the reason my grandparents loved this house."

It was what his grandmother would say to everyone when they saw all her grandchildren staying with them. Janet twisted her face in disapproval, but Julian wasn't changing his mind. And if his grandfather came back from Florida and had a problem with it, then he'd deal with the repercussions. What difference did it make letting Asher have a nice time?

He watched them go and felt a little bit of disappointment. It had been nice to see new people in the house. Not that he minded Janet—he loved her like family, actually—but having noise from other people and having a child's energy in the house again was nice.

When he followed Janet into the kitchen to grab something to drink, she turned around to face him before heading into her office.

"Don't you have enough problems?" Janet asked.

Her directness shook Julian. She didn't sugarcoat what he was. A huge problem.

"I guess."

"Why are you going to mess around with this young woman's life?" she said.

And it made Julian take a step back. He tried his hardest not to be defensive. What would Father Michael say right now? You have to stand in the light to get out of the shadow.

"I'm not trying to hit on her," he said. "I just wanted to be helpful. I'm trying to help."

"You didn't take that upstairs like you said." Janet pointed to the figure. "And that's how you treat women. You say one thing and do another. Stephanie isn't one you can play around with."

He looked down at the action figure on the counter. He had promised Asher, yet he was getting a drink for himself here. Would he have just left it and lost it in the meantime? Is that how he treated people, too? Or was that the old Julian?

Who was he kidding? He was the old Julian.

"I want to change," he said, meeting Janet's eyes. "Seriously, I want to do things that are helpful."

Janet's eyebrows rose in doubt. "You know I love your family," Janet said. "And this job."

He nodded, waiting for the bomb she was about to drop.

"But sitting on the sidelines, watching you fall apart, was hard." She stopped as emotion caught in her voice. To Julian's surprise, Janet's eyes moistened. "Someone should've told you the word 'no' years ago."

He gave Janet a half smile. "You certainly did."

She let out a laugh. "Hardly enough." She sniffled and drew in her tears, getting serious again. "Don't go out there and try to fix your pain with someone else."

He let out a laugh. "That's not what tonight was."

"Then why did you do all this?" Janet asked point blank. "Why have her bring her son? Why play with him upstairs?"

"Because I wanted to?" He almost didn't believe it himself. Why had he?

"I've seen dozens of women come in and out of this house hoping and praying they'll break into that heart of yours, only to be forgotten in the kitchen like that action figure," She pointed to the figure.

Julian quickly picked it up. "I'm taking it upstairs right now."

"There's a reason why they tell people to put on their oxygen masks before helping someone else," Janet said, thickly laying on the advice. "If you don't take care of yourself first, you won't be able to help anyone else."

# CHAPTER 7

*A*sher didn't fall asleep until close to 10:45, which was too late for a school night but also way past her own bedtime. Being up this late, on this rare occasion, revealed just how late the rest of the LaBelles came in on a Thursday night.

"What are you doing up?" Will asked as he stumbled through the door.

She could smell the booze from the recliner.

"I just got home from work," she said, needing a few minutes to decompress before going to bed.

"The diner's open this late?" Will had forgotten about her going to the Abbotts.

"I went to my new job."

Will grabbed a beer, plopped onto the couch and grabbed the remote. "How's Jules these days?"

She closed the thickest binder, which sat on her lap. "I forgot he went by Jules as a kid."

"Not anymore?" Will asked, turning on the television. He flipped to the sports channel. "Does he go by Julian Windsor McDuck Snotty Pants Abbott?" This only made Will laugh at himself.

"What are you even saying?" She picked up the binder and got up. She'd read the rest in bed.

"Has he hit on you yet?" Will asked.

If she had an ounce of confidence, she might have thought Julian was hitting on her after being so kind all night. Never in the history of being a single mother had a handsome man offered to hang out with Asher just to be nice. Not even Asher's dad. Gabe usually did that in order to get something in return. Or for her to thank him for watching his own kid.

"No," she said.

"Just you wait. He can't help himself." Will shook his head.

She threw a look at him. "That's not even funny."

"I'm joking." He raised his hands up.

"Where's Dad?" she asked, checking her phone's time to see if the clock in the living room was working.

"He's probably out with the guys," Will said before sipping from his beer.

It felt late, but what did she know? She was usually asleep by this point. She stood up to go to bed when she saw a car pull up outside the house. Her father sat on the passenger side.

"He must've had quite a bit to drink at bowling," she said, looking out the window. He opened the door, and Stephanie saw a woman sitting behind the wheel. "Who's that?"

Will, who was watching *Sports Center*, didn't even look up. "Probably Bonnie."

"Bonnie?" Stephanie hadn't heard of a Bonnie. "Who's Bonnie?"

That's when she saw her father kiss Bonnie.

"She's kind of his new girlfriend," Will said.

"Wow." She said, as she saw her father kissing a woman other than her mother for the first time in her life. "I guess no one wants to tell me anything."

"He didn't tell me either," Will said, apparently okay with being left in the dark.

"Then how do you know?" she asked, a bit peeved.

"I accidentally ran into them one time," he said.

"And you didn't tell me?" Stephanie couldn't believe her brother didn't think to tell her.

"You've been kind of cranky for the past few years," Will said, staring directly at the television.

Stephanie's jaw dropped. "A few *years*, I've been cranky?"

She was about to lay into Will when the front door opened and her father entered. He walked in smiling to himself but then saw Stephanie. He looked like a deer caught in headlights.

"Who's your friend?" she asked, forcefully bobbing her foot up and down.

"She's someone from bowling." Her father looked at Will, who shrugged.

"You want to tell us about her?" Stephanie wanted to give her father the speech he'd given her when he caught her dating.

"I wasn't going to tell you until she was ready to meet you," he said rationally. "But if you must know, her name is Bonnie. I've known her for some time now, and we've just started talking, as you all say."

She didn't say that, because Stephanie couldn't remember the last time she talked with a man. She thought about tonight and Julian. Had she mistaken his politeness for hitting on her?

She was pathetic. She had only been with Gabe for a few years before things fell apart. She barely understood him, much less other guys. Julian was probably just being nice to her.

"Is she ready to meet us?" Stephanie asked, almost nervous at the idea of her father dating someone. Would that mean she'd have to move out if they got serious? What if she wasn't ready to move out?

"I didn't ask her tonight," her father said. He shrugged and then walked away into the kitchen.

Stephanie almost went in for more questions but stopped herself. She'd respect her father's privacy. Maybe he'd learn from her how to set boundaries.

"Well, that's great, Dad," she said, but she had so many questions. Who was this Bonnie? Did she have any children? Had she been married? How old was she?

Then, a thought popped into her head. "Is that the woman from church?"

The same woman who had sung in the choir with their mother.

"Yes," her father said. He shut off the light in the kitchen. "Good night."

She guessed that was all her father would talk about tonight.

"Night," Will said from the couch.

"Night, Dad." Stephanie got up herself. "Night, Will."

She didn't wait for a response, taking Janet's bag of binders and heading to her room. She had studying to do. She first checked in on Asher, tucking him in again. Her baby boy had passed out with Optimus Prime stuffed under his pillow.

"That can't be very comfortable," she said quietly, smiling at her silly little boy.

She thought about how happy he had been to have a person to play with. She could only imagine what kind of kid he would be if Gabe had been that kind of dad. The one that played with Transformers. Not one that dragged him around and only did what he wanted to do. Gabe could be a good dad, at times, but he usually just thought about himself. At this point, it'd been months, if not years since Gabe had just picked Asher up and done dad things with him.

She picked up the binder, ready to change her train of thought. She opened the cover of *Holidays*, to a table of contents. Each chapter listed the months of the year, starting with January. December was at the very back. What would it be like for Asher to have a family that cataloged their special events to make them absolutely perfect?

She went straight to the Christmas section.

Stephanie had only met Corrine Abbott once or twice. Will had to take her everywhere during the summer when her mother had to do errands and couldn't take her along. She had entered the big house a few times, but only stayed in the kitchen. She remembered swimming at their private beach and in their luxurious pool. Mrs. Abbott would come out with cookies and juice for them all, something her mother would have done.

Why hadn't Stephanie decorated for Christmas yet? Her mother would have taken the boxes out of the attic by now.

She put the binder down and walked out of her room and back to the living room, where Will sat watching television.

"Could you take down all the Christmas boxes from the attic?" she asked, but she wasn't really asking.

Will moaned, scrunching his face. "I don't have time."

"You do have time to decorate for your godson's Christmas." She laid on the guilt.

Will finished the last of his beer and shut off the television. "When does this need to happen?"

"The sooner the better," she said, hoping he'd find time by tomorrow.

He harrumphed. "I'm busy."

"Well, you're not busy now." She plucked the empty beer bottle off the side table.

"I'll wake the house." He looked around the quiet room. "Dad's already in bed."

"He can't hear a thing anyway," she said.

"Then you better help me," he said, getting up. He went straight for the stairs.

She smiled to herself as she tiptoed behind him up the stairs. "Do you remember the attic in the Abbott's house?"

"You mean the playroom?" he said.

"It's like a childhood dream come true."

"It was." Will didn't add more, which disappointed her. She wanted to talk about the house and the Abbotts, but she also didn't want to start in on why she shouldn't work for people like that.

"Is Jules living at the house now?" Will asked as he opened the door to the attic.

"Mm-hmm," she said, quietly going up the wooden stairs. "I think so."

"I heard something like that, but I haven't seen him around," Will observed, just like herself. Julian had been a ghost in Blueberry Bay if he had been living here as long as Janet had said.

"He's been here for a year."

Will's eyes bulged at the information. "I haven't seen him at the bars once."

She hadn't signed an NDA, but she was sure she would once her salary started. She decided to keep what Janet had told her about Julian's sobriety to herself. "He looks good."

Will made a face. "Mark my words: he'll be hitting on you."

She didn't tell him about Asher and the Transformers; she just quietly walked over to the few boxes of decorations the LaBelle family had stored away. Not a whole barn's worth, but enough to fill her childhood Christmas dreams.

"Will you be home tomorrow?" she asked Will as they picked up some boxes.

He nodded. "Are we going to have to get a tree?"

"Two or so," she said.

"Two or so?" He scrunched his forehead.

She headed down the stairs, carefully looking at the steps. "One for us and a few for the Abbotts."

# CHAPTER 8

*J*ulian sat in front of his computer, wondering what his life would be like in a year. He'd never really thought about the future before becoming sober, but now, he spent a lot of time looking forward, hoping for easier times, simpler times. He wondered whether he wanted to get married and if he'd ever find someone he loved again. He thought about having children and whether he'd be a good parent. He thought about whether he was wasting away in Maine, hiding from his demons, or if he should return to the city and get back on the saddle again, as his father liked to put it.

The door to the lounge swung open to Oliver rushing through.

"There you are," Oliver said, coming into the room.

Julian hadn't even heard his brother arrive. "When did you get here?"

Oliver dropped onto the couch with the biggest, widest smile Julian had ever seen.

His stomach dropped. Something major was about to happen.

"I'm not supposed to tell anyone yet," he said, rubbing his hands together. "But I have to tell you."

Julian knew exactly what he was about to say. Oliver and Muriel were having a baby.

"I'm going to be a dad!" he laughed out. His excitement was palpable.

"That's amazing!" Julian said, shutting his computer and going over to his brother. He embraced him. "That's great news."

"We just found out, so Muriel wants to wait until Christmas to tell everyone." Oliver looked like a kid opening presents on Christmas Day. "But I had to tell someone!"

Julian smiled; he had been that someone. Maybe a year ago, he wouldn't have been.

"We're thinking if it's a boy, we should name him Max," Oliver said.

That made Julian smile. "The old man would love that."

Oliver couldn't contain his excitement. "I know."

"That's really great, man," Julian said. But without acknowledging it, something seismic had shifted. Like the day Oliver had left for prep, leaving Julian alone at the Abbott household and experiencing this whole new life without him. Now, his older brother was married and about to become a father. He was at a whole different level of life than Julian.

Julian felt like he was in the gutter of life. He didn't necessarily have anything to show for his work other than the debris left behind from the storms he'd gone through. All that was left was wreckage, clogging up his flow. Would things change or would he stay in this perpetual state of sadness?

"I still can't believe it!" Oliver clapped his hand on his knees.

"Yeah, that's really incredible."

Hopefully, he'd get there.

"I was going to ask if we could have Christmas here," Oliver said. "Like Grandma used to do. Do you think Janet will be able to get it ready?"

"Why don't you just ask her?" Julian asked.

Oliver looked over his shoulder before saying, "She's been really honest lately, and I'm afraid of what she'll say."

"You're afraid of Janet?" Julian laughed at his brother. But he wasn't running into Janet's office and demanding her to do it. Julian didn't want to have the house decorated for Christmas. Just another reminder of how alone he was. "I figured you'd want your own Christmas at your own place."

Would he be included? Would he be included anywhere? Even his parents did their own thing most of the time, forgetting he didn't have his own family. They just assumed he'd go to Maine like he usually did. But it had only been Oliver and his grandfather over the past couple of years.

"What did we do last year?" Julian asked, trying to remember.

"I got married." Oliver's eyebrows rose at the clear faux pas. "And you were in…"

*Rehab.* Julian thought back, and like a Mack truck slamming into him, memories from a year ago became as clear as day.

"Lots has changed in a year," Oliver said, matching his thoughts.

A year ago, Julian had to leave the facility he was staying in for the wedding but had returned that night because he couldn't trust himself.

He still didn't.

Tears stung his eyes at the thought of what Janet had said. What if his grandfather dies? He'd be all alone at that point. Oliver had Muriel. Cora had Brandon. His parents had their toxic relationship. His friends hadn't even called him since he'd left rehab. Julian was all alone.

"Janet hired a new house manager," he said.

"That's good," Oliver said, checking his phone and stuffing it into his pocket. "When's Gramps getting back from Florida?"

"In a week," Julian said. He could tell this was a check-in. Oliver wasn't here to hang out or shoot the breeze; he was coming by to see if Julian was staying sober before he went home to his beautiful wife for the rest of the night. And he had good reason to worry. Julian probably would have taken a drink tonight if they hadn't emptied all the liquor bottles.

He should call his sponsor. He could tell his brother he needed him. Father Michael would tell him what to do.

"So, I should probably head out," Oliver said, jabbing his thumb behind him.

"Yeah," Julian said, rubbing his sweaty palms on his pants. "You want to…" Julian didn't know how to socialize now that having a drink was out of the question. "Want to have breakfast this weekend?"

Oliver stood, stretching. "Sure. That sounds good."

But the two didn't make definite plans. He was almost sure it would be pushed off because Oliver would be busy. He had a full-time teaching job, a new wife, a home, and was about to become a dad.

"Does her family not do Christmas at their house?" he asked. He could remember something from last year.

"Oh yeah, they'll have something on Christmas day," Oliver said casually, not noticing how Julian's heart plummeted. "But I hoped the house could be decorated like old times and we could have a little thing here. If it's too much, then don't worry about it."

Julian shrugged. "I don't see why not?"

But a million reasons flooded his head. Christmas was synonymous with fun drinks, from a classic Christmas mimosa to the spirit-filled spiced eggnog. From peppermint paddies to whimsical green Grinch cocktails, there was something for everyone, all day long.

It was no surprise Julian had loved this holiday.

Now, he wanted to escape from it.

After he walked Oliver out, he sat at the kitchen table for a long time. He rubbed his hands against the surface thinking about the pile of Asher's toys that had sat on top of it. He kind of wished he had asked Stephanie and Asher to come back sooner.

Janet may think he had a thing for Stephanie, but Julian realized he just had a thing about being lonely.

Just as he was thinking about another of his favorite

Christmas cocktails, light shone through the windows from headlights coming up the drive. He wondered if Oliver had forgotten something.

He looked out the window to see an unfamiliar pickup truck idling at the side door. He looked at the time. Not even five o'clock. Had Janet driven her husband's truck to pick something up?

He walked to the door and saw Will LaBelle sitting in the driver's seat. As he opened it, Stephanie froze at the door as though she were about to knock.

"Hey," he said.

"Hi, Julian." When her eyes met his, she frowned. "Are you alright?"

He shook out of whatever mood lingered and put on as happy of a face as he could. "Yeah, just surprised to see you. Janet's already gone home." He looked at her dark office.

"I tried calling that number you gave me, but nobody picked up," she said, she skated her eyes around the kitchen. "My family and I are about to get our Christmas tree, and I thought I should ask you if you wanted me to order Christmas trees for the house?"

She turned to face the truck. The back window opened, and a sweet little face appeared from behind.

"Hey, Asher." Julian waved and left the house.

"You don't have shoes!" Stephanie said, following him down the dry walkway to the truck.

Asher's face beamed as he held up an Optimus Prime.

"Is that yours?" Julian asked as he reached the truck.

"Mm-hmm," Asher said.

"Wow, he's really cool," Julian said to him. He turned to Will, reaching through the window to shake his hand. "How's it going, man?"

"Good," Will said. "You?"

"Good." Julian gave Will a nod. Hard to believe that their long-term childhood friendship was now just reduced to a few words. He turned back to Asher. "Heard you're going to get a tree?"

Will looked in the rearview mirror.

"You don't have boots on," Asher said.

Julian looked down at his socks. "I better go back inside and get them, huh?"

Asher nodded.

"So, do you want trees for the house?" Stephanie asked.

Julian didn't know what to say. *I can't celebrate the happiest season because I'm a drunk.* "Umm…"

He was certain that if he asked his grandfather, he wouldn't want to bother. The heartbreak of celebrating his beloved wife's holiday might be too much to bear.

Will looked back at Asher, then back to Stephanie.

"I'm sorry," Stephanie said, which confused Julian. Why was she sorry? "Did you want to come and choose?"

"Yeah, come!" Asher raised both arms in the air in celebration. "Mr. Abbott is coming!"

"Julian," he corrected the small boy. "You can call me Julian."

"Jules not fancy enough anymore?" Will said from the front. He sounded like he was joking, but there was heat underneath it.

"Are you coming with us, Jules?" Asher asked Julian.

"His name is Mr. Abbott, Asher," Stephanie said in her motherly tone.

"No, I actually miss people calling me Jules, to be honest," Julian said. Only the people who he felt comfortable around called him that. "It's good to see you, Will."

"Well, Jules," Will said. His right lip curled up. "Do you want to come with us to get your Christmas tree?"

# CHAPTER 9

Stephanie sat in the back seat with Asher, wishing she had read more of those binders before showing up at his house. She knew the last Christmas trees Mrs. Abbott had delivered to the house were four Balsam Pines from the local tree farm on Bear Hill Road. Two trees stood eight and a half feet, one stood twelve, and the grand entrance had a twenty-foot tree.

It felt like a lot of lights. How would one go about putting lights on a twenty-foot tree? The last thing she wanted was to climb a ladder, fall off, and break a hip—or worse.

"I was only going to order trees if you wanted them," Stephanie said. "I just figured I should get the trees since Christmas is only a few weeks away. I started reading the binders last night and noticed that your grandmother ordered the trees months before now, so I wanted to make sure I could at least get something decent at this time of the season."

She realized she had begun rambling and hadn't even let Julian respond.

Julian turned to face her from the front passenger seat. "That sounds good, yeah."

But she wondered if she had overstepped or if she wasn't

supposed to burden him with the trivial details of how his family's house ran.

"Does your whole family still come?" she asked.

"Hmm..." Julian shrugged. "My grandfather, maybe my brother and his family, but I don't know if anyone else will come."

"Do you think I should order four trees?" she asked, hoping she wasn't making a substantial first mistake. She started running numbers in her head. If she messed things up, the price would be more than her weekly salary.

"Yeah, Oliver wanted to do Christmas like old times with his wife's family," he said, returning to face the front. "Did you hear he got married?"

Will made a face. "I was at the wedding."

"Oh, right," Julian said, looking out the window. "I forgot. I still can't believe he's married."

Will nodded. "He's pretty well-liked around these parts. Everyone loves the Abbotts over at the school."

"Mrs. Abbott's nice," Asher said.

Julian shifted to face Asher. "Is she your teacher?"

Asher shook his head. "She's a third-grade teacher, but her students are our big buddies."

"Ah," Julian said. "She's pretty nice."

"Yeah," Asher agreed. "And pretty."

"Asher." Stephanie couldn't help but giggle.

"What?" He held up his hands like he didn't understand what cute and innocent thing he had done to make her laugh. "Uncle Will told me to tell him about all the pretty teachers."

"Will!"

"Only the pretty *single* teachers, whose names start with Ms. Isn't that what I said, buddy? Not the Mrs. teachers."

"Oh." Asher thought for a second. "Ms. Smith is really pretty."

Will looked through the rearview mirror at Asher. "Is she a first-grade teacher or the lunch lady?"

"She's the kindergarten teacher, Uncle Will!" Asher smacked

his forehead as though Will was a complete idiot for not knowing the entire staff directory of Blueberry Bay School.

"Is she new?" Will asked seriously, which made her laugh, and she saw that Julian had started to laugh, too.

She couldn't help but laugh at something so stupid yet entertaining. She didn't feel as weird around Julian when Will was around. It had been so long. It felt like when they were kids.

"Isn't it funny it's the three of us again?" Will said, turning on his blinker to turn into the farm.

Julian let out a chuckle. "I didn't think we'd ever get Stephanie into a car with the two of us again after that drive down Route 1 when she turned sixteen."

Will let out a screech and then started slapping the wheel. "I completely forgot about that."

Stephanie unbuckled as Will came to a parking spot. "Well, I haven't."

But she had forgotten about that drive along the ocean in Julian's father's Porsche.

"I still can't believe we did that," Will said.

"Did what, Uncle Will?" Asher said, getting out of his booster seat.

"Nothing," Stephanie said quickly before one of the guys told her secret. She'd driven before she got her license at the persistence of Will and Julian. "You two always did the dumbest things."

"Nuh-uh," Will said, bringing her back to being a teenager again, arguing about everything with him.

"We did the coolest stuff together," Julian said back at her.

Not much had changed. Julian always took Will's side. She smiled at him before taking Asher's mittened hand. "Let's go pick out a Christmas tree."

She walked ahead, but Asher lagged, pulling her to slow down. "Uncle Will and Jules are still at the truck."

Julian jogged across the parking lot to catch up and pointed to the small log cabin that housed the registers and baked

79

goods being sold at the farm. "Should we get some hot cocoa first?"

Asher's eyes widened in delight, and they looked at her. He grabbed hold of her stomach with both hands. "Can I please?"

"Can I?" Will said from behind.

Stephanie laughed at the ridiculousness and the pleasure of it all. "Let's all get some!"

Asher cheered, raising his arms into the air. "Woo-hoo!"

He began skipping ahead to the log cabin, pulling Stephanie along.

Four hot cocoas and four Christmas cookies later, they walked down the rows of trees, checking out their sizes, holding them up to examine, and spinning them around to check out their full profiles.

"That's too skinny," Stephanie said, moving quickly through the six-foot trees.

Will picked out another six-footer and tapped its trunk on the frozen ground.

"I think we need something smaller for our house," she said.

They continued through the rows of trees, and she couldn't help but glance at Julian. She hadn't allowed herself to look at him, but the young man she had spent nights dreaming about marrying still could be seen under that five o'clock shadow and chiseled jawline.

He probably doesn't remember teasing her like he did, making her think he might like her back. He certainly didn't remember when he'd stuck up for her at the beach when those rotten girls had given her a hard time. And he didn't remember the night when she'd been at the bar and he'd tried kissing her. No, he definitely didn't remember that. She hadn't told anyone about that. Not even Will.

Gabe had been stationed away and "needed space," which really meant he didn't want to be tied down with a wife and kid. It had been the first time the roller-coaster relationship of on-again, off-again had plummeted off the rails. The pain and hurt had caused her to go out with Will and his friends, but she'd mostly sat at the bar alone, drowning in her own misery until Julian had come in.

Looking back, she should have noticed how loose and easy-going he had been. He hadn't seemed drunk; if anything, he had been…merry. Everyone had been that night, even her dad. It had been the annual lobsterman Christmas party. She didn't even know why she had gone. It wasn't a thing she had attended before or again. But there she was, talking to Julian Abbott, reminiscing of the good old days and enjoying herself for the first time in a long time.

Like now.

"There it is," she said, stopping in front of the most perfect tree she had ever seen.

Julian tilted his head to get a better look, then grabbed its trunk, holding it upright for her to see.

"It's puny," Will said, walking beside her.

"I love it!" Asher jumped up and down. "It's perfect."

It was perfect. She winked at Asher and squeezed his free hand three times. Her *I love you* signal. He squeezed back three times. The tree looked exactly like his bedtime book's Christmas tree. "I thought so."

Will tried getting Asher to pick a taller and fuller tree, but nothing would make Asher change his mind. He loved his Christmas tree.

With a fresh cut, Stephanie and Julian ordered the trees for the Abbott house. Will put the tree in the back of his truck and they all got in.

"I can take you home, or you could join us for dinner," Will said to Julian, putting the truck in reverse. "I mean, if you don't have anything better to do. Stephanie made lobster bisque."

It had been her mother's tradition when they'd put up the tree. "Our father will be there."

"I've got a twelve-pack of some swanky IPA," Will said.

"Yeah, sure, that sounds great." Julian tapped his fingers on the car door.

Stephanie's heart started racing as sudden panic interrupted the joyous afternoon. Technically, it was the second day she had worked for the Abbotts, and now her brother was about to ruin his year of sobriety. How was she going to fix it?

She rattled off all the possibilities of trying not to embarrass Julian. She didn't know much about those who got clean from an addiction, but she was certain he didn't need a mother hen telling him what to do.

She should call Janet.

When they reached home, Asher jumped out of the truck, following the guys as they carried the tree to the garage.

"We're going to have to use the chainsaw!" Will shouted out in joy.

Asher cheered the same way he had when Will had used the chainsaw the year before. "I'll get the masks."

Stephanie laughed as she tried to devise a good excuse to talk to Will alone. She'd ask Will to help her in the kitchen. But as soon as Will reached the garage, he walked straight to the old refrigerator plugged in the back.

"Beer?" he asked Julian.

She almost jumped out and smacked the bottle out of Will's hand, but Julian pointed to the house.

"I need to use the bathroom," he said, ignoring the question. "Mind if I use yours?"

"No, no," Stephanie said. "Do you remember where it is?"

Asher grabbed Julian's hand, and Stephanie froze. She hadn't seen Asher warm up to a man besides her brother and father this fast before. Even Gabe had to chip away his shyness when he saw him.

"I'll take you there," Asher said, leading him through the garage to the kitchen door.

"Great, thanks." Julian followed behind the six-year-old,

holding his hand and doing everything Asher said, including closing the door behind him.

"He's a bossy little man," she said, turning to Will. "So, he's sober."

"Yeah, because he's six," Will said, scrunching his forehead.

"No, Julian. He's like, gone through rehab," she whispered. "So don't offer him anything to drink."

Will winced. "Why didn't you say something before I offered him a beer?"

"Shush!" she hissed at him. They both looked at the house silently.

She turned back to Will. "How was I supposed to know you would turn into Mr. Rogers and invite my boss over?"

"He was my friend first," he said, crossing his arms. "Besides, I won't offer him anything to drink."

Will put the beer back.

And that was that. Julian came back, the chainsaw left a fresh cut, and the tree was taken into the house.

"What a good-looking tree," her father said from his spot in the living room.

Asher slid into her father's lap and hugged him. "I picked the best one."

"It sure is." Her dad squeezed him tight. Then he looked up and noticed Julian for the first time.

Stephanie braced for a rude comment, but to her surprise, her father got Asher down and stood up with his hand outstretched. "Well, young man, it's good to see you."

For a split second, she swore she saw mist hit Julian's eyes when her father took him into a hug as they shook hands.

"I'm starving," Asher whined from her side.

"Then let's eat!" Stephanie clapped her hands together.

Asher rushed into the kitchen and grabbed the stool so he could reach the plates to set the table. He climbed up onto the counter and pulled open the cabinet door while simultaneously ducking underneath it as it swung out towards him. Julian must have never seen a young boy dangerously perform acrobatic moves to retrieve dinnerware, because he raced from the living room, through the dining room and into the kitchen to swoop Asher up into his very muscular arms to help him.

"Let me help you with that," he said, pulling the plates down with Asher.

"What do you say, Asher?" she said, hoping Julian didn't think she was a reckless mother.

"Thanks," Asher said, hopping out of his arms and onto the floor. He took the plates and continued on his way to setting the table.

Julian laughed. "He's a great kid, Stephanie."

She looked at Asher as he placed the plates her mother had gotten at the Salvation Army and nodded. "He's the best thing I've ever made."

She laughed at herself for saying such a cheesy thing but then looked over to Julian, who was fully staring at her.

"What is it?" she said, brushing her face. "Do I have a chocolate mustache?"

He shook his head. "No, I'm just having a nice time tonight. I'm glad you came by today."

She could feel her cheeks heat up as he kept his stare on her.

"Yeah, it's been fun," she said when the door opened from the garage. Her father came in with a few beers in his hand. "Want one?"

"Dad, no, he doesn't drink!" she said, louder than she had intended.

Julian gave a half smile and no longer met her eyes. "Yeah, I'm good."

She could've kicked herself. What was she thinking answering for him? "I'm sorry. I didn't mean to."

He held up his hand. "It's okay. Seriously."

Asher stood at the table. "I'm hungry!"

Julian laughed as he walked into the dining room.

As Stephanie filled a pitcher of water, Will grabbed the soap and started washing his hands. "Well, that didn't take long,"

"What didn't take long?" she said, stepping aside so he could use the water.

"Julian hitting on you." Will ran his hands under the stream.

Stephanie let out a holler of a laugh. Then, she swatted a dish towel at him. "He's just my boss."

"Sure," Will said, turning off the water. "Whatever you say."

But as she saw Asher pull his chair closer to sit next to Julian, she had a weird fluttering feeling she hadn't felt in a very long time.

# CHAPTER 10

*J*ulian didn't think he had a thing for Stephanie. Well, not until that moment. But maybe subconsciously, he wanted to go back to his childhood and have some sort of connection to Will again. After all, Will had been the only person from before he had started drinking who liked him for who he was. He and Oliver had gotten along fine, but they weren't best friends like he was with Will. They'd been inseparable any time Julian had been lucky enough to be in Maine. They'd be together from the second he'd get there to the moment he'd have to leave. And he'd be at the LaBelle's the whole time.

But then they never hung out again. Until now.

He was surprised to hear that Oliver had even invited Will to the wedding. That's why he hadn't noticed him, though he'd been completely out of it at that point anyway. He couldn't even remember his speech that night. But he hadn't been looking for Will, because Will hadn't even been friends with Oliver. It must be a new connection. A new friendship that Julian wasn't a part of.

He was even more surprised that Will had included him in their day. That's what he had always done. Julian had only dared to invite him to his house maybe a handful of times, too embarrassed that his parents would say something off-key and hurt their friendship somehow.

Will hadn't seemed to notice the off-the-cuff comments about how his mother had wanted him to come to the side door like a house worker instead of a regular guest. Or how they'd done a sweep with their eyes on his clothes. And the worst offense had gone to his father, who had called him *fishy boy* because he would frequently smell of the day's catch even after a long shower.

"Do you still catch the sea gold?" Julian hoped they still did.

"Sure do," Will said, stringing the last of the lights around the tree.

"I still think about it," Julian said. Every time he'd sat in his old office building, he'd had a great view of the water and always wondered what life was like for Will, just sitting out in the middle of the water, nothing for as far as the eye could see.

"Come out anytime," Will said.

"How 'bout tomorrow?"

Julian said it as a joke, but Will just shrugged and said, "Okay."

Will looked at Stephanie, who frowned with disapproval. "I mean, not tomorrow, since I have to babysit. But maybe another day."

"Can I go fishing?" Asher asked.

The three LaBelle adults looked at each other, having a silent conversation.

"You want to go out on the boat, buddy?" Will's forehead creased. "You don't like the boat, I thought."

Asher held the star in his hands, patiently waiting for his moment to place it on top of the tree.

"I don't mind it," Asher said.

They all laughed.

"You cried the whole time you were on it," Will said, shaking his head.

"Maybe he's ready now," Brian said. He shook his fist at Asher, a twinkle of pride in his eye. "A man just goes out there and pushes through the headwinds."

Julian smiled down at the young man. The kid had more guts at six than he did at thirty.

Will turned to Stephanie. "Do you mind if I take him out on the boat?"

Stephanie didn't answer for a while, which made him think she wouldn't let him, but she put her hands on her hips, facing Asher. "You have to wear a life vest."

"I will." Asher stood straight like a soldier, pulling back his shoulders and puffing out his little chest.

"And you have to listen to your uncle and Mr. Abbott. I don't want you to go anywhere near the traps." She took a pause, catching a glance at the two men. Just before she was about to say something, Asher interrupted her.

"Jules," Asher threw out.

She closed her mouth, smiling at her son. "Jules." She jabbed her thumb behind her. "Let's get that star up."

Asher started bouncing up and down as Will picked him up and put him on his shoulders. "Let's get you over there."

Asher held on to the star that had seen much better days. Most of the gold paint and glitter had faded away, and one of the corners had a chip. Asher placed it on the tree crookedly. But as the Abbotts cheered Asher on and acted as Julian had been there all along through the years, he thought it was the most beautiful Christmas tree he had ever seen, and he became conscious that he felt happier than he had in a very long time.

Maybe since the last time he'd come here.

When the star sat perfectly in place, Stephanie handed Asher more ornaments and then passed one to Julian.

"Oh, I'm fine. I don't need to decorate your tree," he said, holding up his hand in refusal.

But she didn't move. She pushed the ornament into his palm.

"You made this," she said.

He picked up the wooden piece with tiny shells glued on. Gold, red, and blue glitter covered the entire thing. Its hook was a pipe cleaner. On the back the name "Jules" was engraved, along with the year.

He didn't even remember making it, but the ornament had his childhood signature. "I can't believe you still have this."

He walked over to the tree next to Asher.

"Where should I place it?" he asked.

Asher pointed to the second-highest branch. "Right there."

And the back of his eyes began to sting.

"Alright, let's get a family photo," Stephanie said. "You too, Julian."

She turned around before Julian could get himself together. "I need to run to the restroom."

He walked away before she even responded, his eyes cast to the ground, trying to hide his sudden outburst of emotion.

He was such an idiot! And now she probably thought he had bathroom issues. How could he have made things worse? She must think he was a raging alcoholic, telling her father not to give him a beer. He wondered if Janet had told her about him. Or had it spread across town that the youngest Abbott was a complete lush?

"Get yourself together," he said into the mirror. The person he stared at looked old and weary, unsure about life and what his next steps should be. Nothing like the lush who had owned the space he occupied. He didn't cry when seeing a sweet family moment. He took his moments.

He knew he'd most likely win Stephanie over if he had a drink. Something about having a drink in him allowed him to become a complete Romeo with women. He never got turned down *until* he was sober.

And then they never wanted him.

One drink and he'd be telling her sweet nothings, all the things she wanted to hear, and he'd adapt into what she wanted in a man for that moment, like a chameleon. It had been a way to fit in, but it had become an art form by the end of his drinking tenure.

When he opened the bathroom door to return to the living room, Stephanie stood at the end of the hall. She couldn't hide the worry across her face.

"Are you alright?" she asked.

He put on the smile that charmed clients. "Absolutely. Just needed to freshen up."

Stephanie looked relieved and put her hands together. "Oh, good. I was worried that the bisque might have made you ill." She looked back at the living room. "Then let's take that picture."

As he walked into the room, Asher still hung on Will's shoulders, the tree had been lit up, and Brian stood next to them.

"Hurry up, Mom!" Asher said, holding on to Will's hair like it was a rein.

"Dude! Watch the hair." Will play smacked Asher's little hands, sending the boy into a fit of laughter.

"I can take it," Julian said, holding his hand toward Stephanie's phone.

"No, we all did this," she said, putting her phone on a stool and placing a book behind it to stand it up. She bent over, peering into the screen. "Dad, move over just a little to the right."

She walked over to Julian, put her hands on his shoulders, and dragged him to where she wanted him. Then she ran back to the camera, pressed the button, and returned to the group.

"Say Merry Christmas in three, two, one," she said through her smile.

"Merry Christmas!" they all shouted.

Except for Julian, who was certain that if he talked right then, even just a simple "Merry Christmas," he might cry, and he wasn't sure if he could pull himself together.

As soon as the picture was taken, he stepped away from the tree, focusing on the door.

"Thanks so much for a wonderful night. It's been great being back here with all of you, but I really should get going." He didn't even break his stride before reaching the front door. "Thank you so much."

"Don't you need a ride?" Will asked.

The group's faces said it all. He was acting like a maniac.

He shook his head, forgetting he had driven over in Will's truck.

"Let me put Asher to bed, and I can take you home," Stephanie said.

"No, I want to come," Asher said.

"Sure, but you need to wear boots."

"Aww, do I have to?" he said.

"What if our car breaks down?" she said. "It's winter. You need your boots."

Julian smiled, remembering when Asher had asked him where his boots were. "I don't want to be any trouble."

"Will basically stole you from your night," she teased, and she gave him a wink. "I just need to grab my purse."

"I asked him," Will said from the couch.

When Stephanie came back, she said, "You two can take those boxes back upstairs to the attic."

Will and Brian both made a face.

"But we're just going have to bring them back down at the end of the season," Will complained.

"Yup. Your point?" she said, acting as if she didn't understand.

Will rolled his eyes, then waved to Julian. "Have a nice night, man. You still in for tomorrow?"

Julian had almost forgotten. Did Will want to take him on the boat? He wasn't sure if he could control his emotions, but he might never get another shot at it again.

"Absolutely," he said.

"Yes!" Asher pulled his elbow behind him in victory.

And Stephanie smiled at him. "Come on, let's go."

They walked outside, and a light snow began to fall.

"Are you sure you don't mind driving?" he asked, hoping the snow wouldn't worsen. Any type of precipitation could create dangerous road conditions.

"I'm a Maine girl," she said, getting into the car. "This is nothing."

Asher entered the backseat, and Julian wondered if he should join him. He felt unworthy of the seat next to someone like Stephanie. She appeared so much wiser than him, as if she had lived a whole other life before this one.

She let the car warm up as she played with the radio. "Let's at least find some Christmas music."

And just like magic, "White Christmas" came on the radio.

"Get out!" She slammed her hand on the wheel, looking into the mirror. "I think Grandma's listening."

Asher held up his finger and said, "I think she helped us pick our tree."

Julian had heard about Mrs. LaBelle's passing. He remembered his grandfather telling him on the phone. He was confident the family had sent flowers.

"I'm so sorry she passed away," he said, wishing now he had attended the funeral. "She always welcomed me into the house like I was one of her own."

Mrs. LaBelle was the kind of mother who had made sure her children treated their guests like honored members of the family. Will always had to sacrifice for Julian to feel welcome. He'd given up his bed when he slept over, he had to do extra chores so he could do things with Julian, and he always had to bring Stephanie along if Mrs. LaBelle had to go somewhere.

Their house had been the refuge he needed throughout his childhood. He was certain that if he hadn't had the LaBelles, he may have turned out much worse than he had.

"She was an amazing woman," he said.

And that's when he noticed the glisten in her eyes. Guess it was that kind of night.

"I'm sorry," he said.

She shook her head, dabbing her eyes with her shirt. "It just sometimes hits me." She sniffled and then laughed. "It's been three years. You'd think I'd be used to it, but it can still just get me, you know, right here."

She patted her chest with her hand and looked at Asher in the rearview.

"I don't think you ever get used to losing your mom." He studied the snow falling on the windshield, wishing he could be honest about his feelings like that.

But that's the thing about being an Abbott. You didn't bother teaching your children emotions. When they'd lost his grandmother, everyone pretended like she had never existed. No one cried in front of one another, not even his grandfather.

As she turned on Main Street, another song came on, and Stephanie turned the dial up on the volume, blasting Mariah Carey's Christmas song as loud as it could go. Every window and tree had been decorated for the holiday. The streetlamps had white lights strung around their posts, with wreaths hanging from them. Window boxes were filled with garland and red bows and ornaments.

As they arrived, the Chipmunks sang about hula hoops, and Asher sang louder than the stereo.

"Thanks again for tonight," he said once Stephanie turned the music down. "I had a great time."

Stephanie nodded. "Us too. It's nice to have you around again."

If Brandon were here, he'd tell Julian to speak his truth. He'd tell her how he enjoyed being a part of things again, how he missed being a bonus LaBelle child, and how his emotions had gotten the better of him because he felt like he belonged again. He'd tell her how grateful he was that she had agreed to become their house manager and how glad he was to have met Asher.

But instead, he asked, "Are you coming back to meet with Janet?" He hoped he didn't sound like a creep.

"Yeah, tomorrow, after my shift," she said.

"Can I come?" Asher asked.

"No, you're going fishing with Uncle Will, remember?" she said, looking at him through the rearview mirror.

"Can I come back another time?" Asher asked, and it tugged at Julian's heart that Asher wanted to come back.

"You can always come and play," Julian said, but he could feel he was coming on thick. Did he sound as desperate to her as he did to himself?

"Maybe I could work with Mommy at your house? Asher asked Julian.

"You have school," Stephanie said.

"I don't want to go to school," Asher whined. His lower lip immediately puckered out. "I hate school."

"Asher, stop that. You love school," she said.

"You don't like school?" Julian asked the boy.

Asher shook his head vehemently. "I hate it."

"But I thought you said your teachers are really nice." Julian furrowed his eyebrows in concern.

"They are, but I don't want to leave Mommy," Asher said, not ashamed of being a momma's boy.

Julian remembered feeling the same way with his mother. When he'd started prep school, he secretly begged his mother to change her mind so he could stay home for high school, but she told him he needed to grow up. "Stop being a momma's boy" may have been her exact words, but in French. She must have thought his French would be too weak for him to understand, but even in a different language, he understood loud and clear.

"You worry your mom might need you?" he asked Asher.

Asher nodded while transforming Optimus's leg. "Yup. She might need me to get something down."

He thought about Asher climbing the counter before dinner. "Yeah, she is pretty short."

"Hey!" Stephanie playfully swiped at Julian's arm with her hand.

And that's when he felt it. The lingering buzzing feeling he got when he liked a girl. When his brain lost focus because of the way her eyes twinkled in the night or how she smelled of vanilla and lavender at the same time.

"I should go." He got out before he did or said anything stupid.

"Say good night to Jules," she said to Asher.

Asher held out his hand for a fist bump. "Good night, Jules!"

As Julian got out, he stopped and said, "Could you just text me when you make it home? The snow seems to be picking up."

"Sure." Stephanie smiled. "Good night, Jules."

As soon as the door closed, Asher called out in his Santa voice, "And to all a goodnight!" The music returned to full volume as Stephanie slowly pulled out of the driveway. He could hear "Jingle Bell Rock" fade away as she drove down the street.

Julian stood out on the front porch thinking about buying a pair of boots, watching them until they were completely out of sight.

# CHAPTER 11

S tephanie took a shower after working at the diner and put on the best winter business outfit she could find. Winter season wasn't her best season. She always felt a bit frumpy in sweaters and jeans. She could never find the perfect fit with any of it, especially with the new styles.

But today, she would settle on the smart sweater-and-slack combo. It was something her mother would wear, and her mom was the smartest woman she had ever known.

"You'll want to freshen the kitchen each season," Janet began as soon as Stephanie had come through the door. She didn't even stop her stride as they walked throughout the house. "On Mondays, we refresh the house for the workweek. Even though Mr. Abbott has been officially retired from the Senate for ten years, he still *behaves* like he's headed to the office. Business casual is always worn during the week. And formal wear, especially if you work at night, during the weekends. You might want to invest in both formal and casual wear. I shop at Talbots."

Stephanie thought she might have been a mixture of both, but by the way Janet examined her attire, she was certain she wasn't even the latter.

"Let's start upstairs today." Janet scooted right up the staircase like a gazelle, and Stephanie jogged behind her to catch up. "Refresh days are Mondays and Fridays if there are no guests. If there are guests, then each morning, I do a quick refresh and one major refresh on Tuesday and Thursday."

When Janet reached the top step, she stopped, and the stairs opened to a long balcony overlooking the grand front hall. Stephanie looked out, imagining the twenty-foot tree they had managed to order.

"It's Colonel Mustard in the front hall with the knife," Stephanie teased, but Janet wasn't impressed.

"Oh, did Julian tell you?"

Lines creased between Janet's eyes. "Tell me what?"

"We ordered Christmas trees," Stephanie said, proud of her important first accomplishment. She smiled at the memory of last night already being one of the best in her life. She'd never seen all of the men in her life so happy. Even her dad had a smile on his face.

Janet looked surprised by all of it. "You ordered trees?"

Stephanie nodded as she held the shiny wood railing, staring out at the grand hall.

"Does it go here?" She pointed down below where she imagined the tree would go.

"Yes." Janet's worry lines increased even more, morphing into something that looked like a bit of shock and horror. "Did Julian say he wanted the trees?"

"Ahh…" Stephanie rolled the events back through her mind. She had been so busy working, decorating for Christmas, cooking lobster bisque, and gathering everyone together that she couldn't remember whether he'd wanted the trees. Had he ever said so?

She couldn't remember, but she did remember him standing there while they picked them out, and the looks he kept sneaking at her throughout the night.

"I was hoping he'd want to decorate for Oliver and his new wife," Janet said. "He's been dragging his feet about it."

Stephanie said nothing, still unsure if she had forced Julian to get the trees.

"The Abbotts buy their linens through Blueberry Bay Linens," Janet said, as she returned to the training. "You'll find all the information in the—"

"Binder," Stephanie finished for her.

"Yes, the binder," Janet said.

"You have eight formal guest rooms but could sleep up to thirty-six comfortably if all the rooms are used efficiently." Stephanie recited from the binder. "Fourteen bathrooms, including the two master baths, are the only rooms to get refreshed daily."

"You've done your homework," Janet said.

It's the one thing Stephanie had excelled at in life. School.

She'd aced everything, including studying. She had loved taking notes, organizing her work, and learning. Learning something new, even the binders for a house manager, excited her.

"I didn't realize how many different vendors you have to be in contact with for a place like this." Stephanie had counted over forty businesses and companies that helped run the house that sat along the cliffs of the Atlantic Ocean.

"Wait, did you come here last night?" Janet suddenly looked horrified, confused, and then back to horrified.

"Yes…" Stephanie wished she had called Janet before doing any of that.

"And he seemed okay with it?" Janet's face continued to twist.

"Yes…" Should she pack her bags?

"Well, Stephanie, I didn't think you could handle Julian." Janet now looked impressed. "But I've been trying to put a Christmas tree in this house for five years."

Now Stephanie looked horrified. "Why didn't you tell me that before giving me the"—she used her fingers to air quote— "house Bible?"

"I honestly didn't think you'd read through it before Christmas." Janet shook her head. "Especially not in a few nights."

"Well, I'm trying to do a good job." Stephanie wondered if she was. "You think I should ask Max Abbott about the trees?"

Janet shook her head. "It'll do this family some good to see their old traditions. They've been so caught up in all the things that are going wrong, they've forgotten what's right about this family."

Stephanie couldn't stop thinking about that saying for the rest of the night. Had she been so caught up in all the wrong in her life that she couldn't focus on all the right?

She had a very supportive family, even though they drove her crazy and acted like children themselves half the time.

By the time they finished refreshing the upstairs, the front door to the house opened, and in came Julian, Will, and Asher.

"Hi, Mom!" Asher said from the first floor.

"Asher?" Stephanie's heart immediately began to flutter in alarm. "Is everything alright?"

"We caught some lobsters!" Asher pointed to Will, who held up an ice box with Julian.

"Come on, Janet. Dinner's on me tonight!" Julian shouted from down below.

Janet looked down at the three men and, under her breath, said, "What did he do today?"

It turned out the day of catching lobsters had been a success. Asher had loved the water and Julian enjoyed it too, same as he remembered loving it as a kid.

"We're cooking dinner," Julian said from below.

As Stephanie and Janet continued reviewing the different responsibilities of refreshing the house, such as replacing all the flowers, linens, and towels throughout, Julian and Will cooked the lobster and Asher set the table in the kitchen.

While Janet described how the towels were folded and placed in the linen closet, which was as big as Asher's bedroom, Stephanie could hear laughter and shouting coming from the kitchen.

"And get used to this," Janet said.

"What?" Stephanie asked, putting a towel back in its place, folded in thirds.

"Julian's little gatherings." Janet rolled her eyes, unimpressed. "Before he became sober, these would happen all the time. He'd bring people around the house, mostly women, to continue the fun."

"Oh." Stephanie thought about the *women* part. It shouldn't bother her that her boss, and her brother's renewed friend, had women come to *his* house. "What do you keep on hand to entertain?"

"It used to be liquor. Now..." Janet shrugged. "I guess that's up to you to figure out."

"Right," Stephanie said, placing another towel in the correct spot on the shelf. She wanted to ask Janet if she thought she was the right person for the job. She wondered if Julian had hired her because of Will. Pointing it out to Janet wouldn't do any good at this point. She had less than a week before the senior Mr. Abbott returned. She'd have to make herself the right person for the job.

That's when she heard the doorbell.

"I've got it!" Julian called out.

Stephanie looked through the linen door to the balcony and heard a woman's voice.

"We should see if they need help," Janet said, putting all the linen in her arms on the table in the middle of the room.

Stephanie followed her downstairs to see more people in the kitchen. Oliver and his wife Muriel had just arrived. Stephanie had seen the couple at school and around town quite a bit.

"Janet, I heard you're leaving?" Muriel said sadly, moving towards Janet to give her a big hug. "What are we going to do without you?"

"Well, you've got Stephanie now, and she's going to do just fine." Janet gave Stephanie a wink, and it was precisely the kind of affirmation that Stephanie had wanted all day.

Stephanie went straight over to Muriel and shook her a hand. "Mrs. Abbott, it's so nice to see you. Asher, say hi to Mrs. Abbott."

Asher suddenly turned shy and lifted his hand. "Hi, Mrs. Abbott."

"Nice to see you too. I didn't know you were taking over for Janet." Muriel looked to Oliver, who shrugged innocently.

"Don't look at me, I didn't know either" he said.

"Are you here for dinner?" Janet asked.

"We've got enough for Billy, too," Julian said from his spot at the stove. "He'll be joining us soon."

Janet's face was stricken. "You invited my husband, Billy?"

"Yeah," Julian said. "We ran into him at the docks."

Will let out a laugh. "He was complaining to Julian for taking you away at night."

"Billy was complaining about his dinner? Because I made him plenty to eat!" Janet put her hands on her hips.

Julian shook his head. "He just misses you."

"Well, that's okay," Janet said, her demeanor suddenly softer around the men.

Stephanie watched as the boys took over the kitchen, boiling the water for the lobster, and preparing the rest of the food.

"Did you go to the grocery store?" Stephanie asked, looking at all the ingredients lying on the counter.

"We ran to the market"—Will paused to drink a bottle of water— "and grabbed some stuff."

After work, Will usually had a beer. She couldn't remember a night he hadn't grabbed a beer before even saying hello to everyone or came home from the bar already tipsy.

Asher watched as Julian rubbed the potatoes with oil.

"We're going to make my mom's famous lobster dish," Julian said.

Janet let out a whoop. "Well, it's about time." She opened a drawer, grabbed an apron, and threw another to Stephanie. "You might as well learn this recipe, too."

Muriel grabbed an apron as well and joined the group in the kitchen. Stephanie reintroduced herself to Oliver, Julian's older brother. She hadn't talked to him other than saying hi as a young girl, but like Julian, he was friendly and easy to talk to.

"Do you like living here full-time?" she asked him, wondering how the summer kid had become a local.

"I love it," Oliver said. "Wish Julian would just stay already."

Stephanie snuck a glance at Julian. She hadn't even thought about that. She had assumed he was staying if he had been here a whole year. What would happen to her position if he wasn't staying at the house? Especially since the senior Abbott was in Florida? Why would they keep her around?

She pushed the thoughts away as she helped with the rest of the prep. When she had first started working with Janet, she wasn't sure if the woman liked the Abbotts. But as Janet helped Julian prep while Will and Oliver teased him, she noticed that Janet behaved very motherly toward the two Abbott boys. When Janet must have thought Stephanie wasn't paying attention, she could hear Janet tell Julian how proud she was that he wanted to put his grandmother's Christmas decorations out.

"You know how much she loved Christmas," Janet said to him.

By the time dinner was ready and Billy had arrived, everyone sat around the table, holding hands, ready to say a prayer.

"I guess this is me," Julian said, lowering his head. Everyone followed his lead. "Dear father..." He paused.

When the silence continued, Stephanie wasn't sure if she should look up or not, but then she heard Asher get off his chair and walk over to where Julian sat.

"It's okay. My mom says it's okay to cry even if you're a boy."

Stephanie looked up and saw Asher hand Julian his napkin.

Julian smiled at her son, his eyes brimming with tears. "Thanks, little man."

On the other side of the table, Janet dabbed her eyes with a napkin.

Julian cleared his throat. "I just wanted to thank everyone for coming tonight. And for taking me out today. It was an adventure of a lifetime." Julian stopped again. "And if I could get a decent blessing out, I'd bless this food and everyone sitting at the table."

"Amen!" Janet said, sniffling.

Muriel clapped as she leaned into Oliver, who patted Julian on the back. "Well said."

With bibs all around the table, they cracked open their lobsters and poured Corrine Abbott's famous white sauce over the broiled tail. The meat melted in her mouth, and conversation flowed as everyone filled their bellies while listening to Janet and Billy talk about their next adventure.

"We're headed down the coast in our boat, and we'll go wherever the wind takes us," Billy said, grabbing Janet's hand at the table.

Stephanie wished she had her mother around or a good girlfriend to talk about everything with later, but all she had were big lobstermen and one little dude. After her mom had passed, it was like she had no one to talk to anymore, even though she lived with her family.

Tonight had been great, but like everything in her life, it would only last for a short time. Janet was leaving in two weeks. Julian wasn't planning on staying longer than he had to. And Will wasn't going to stay forever either. He'd find someone who thought he was as great as she did. It was only a matter of time.

The thought of her future scared Stephanie. In about twelve years, her son would be getting ready to leave home. That was it: twelve years, and all her sacrifices, all the dreams she'd pushed to the side, would no longer matter. And she would be left with no one.

Sure, she'd have a freedom she hadn't ever had before. But she wouldn't end up like her mother, with a household of people at the end of her life. She would be lucky if her father stuck around, but it sounded like he'd already moved on with Bonnie.

"So, Asher, how's the first grade?" Muriel asked him.

Asher frowned. "It's alright."

"It's alright?" Muriel opened her eyes in shock. "You have Mrs. Miller. She's the nicest teacher!"

"I like Mrs. Miller," Asher said, pushing aside a piece of food he didn't want. "It's just that my mom needs me."

Muriel nodded. "I bet she misses you a lot."

Asher nodded.

"Sometimes leaving in morning is hard," Stephanie said, but she knew Muriel had seen Asher's breakdowns when she dropped him off at school.

"I heard leaving for school is hard," Muriel said to him.

"You know Colin, right?" Muriel asked, seriously.

"Yes, he's my reading buddy!" Asher's excitement rose at the mention of his friend.

"He used to get nervous leaving his mom," she said, "and now look at him."

"He doesn't ever look nervous at school," Asher observed.

"That's right." Muriel tapped the table. "Hey, what if Colin met you at the bus stop? He lives just a few blocks away. I'm sure his mom wouldn't mind if he met you at your stop."

Stephanie couldn't believe it. Colin going to the bus stop would solve a lot. "That would be—"

"Awesome," she and Asher said at the same time.

Asher looked at Stephanie with a new excitement for school she hadn't seen before. If anything good came out of working at the Abbott household, it would be this moment right here.

As everyone finished dinner, Stephanie got up to collect plates, and Julian gently put his hand on top of her arm.

"That's okay," he said. "I'll clean up."

Janet's eyes shot over to Stephanie. This must have surprised Janet, because she watched him take the plates and bring them to the sink.

"Stop it, Janet. I do clean up," he said.

She waved her hand at him. "I know you do. It's just nice to see, that's all."

He gave a smile to Stephanie as he took her plate.

"Thanks," she said, almost breathless because she could smell the scent of musk and woodsmoke coming off his shirt. Was she staring at this point?

As everyone helped clear the table, she hoped this wasn't the only time dinner would be so easy. So far, this house manager stuff didn't seem so bad. She could get used to this.

"Are you able to swing by tomorrow night?" Janet asked as she put on her coat.

"Ah…" Stephanie hadn't planned on it.

"We can go over refreshing the rest of the house. The rest of the binders are on my desk." Janet pulled her zipper up fast. Then, she stuffed her head into a knitted hat. "Well, folks, I'll see you tomorrow."

Muriel and Oliver left after that.

"I'll take Asher home with me," Will said as he grabbed Asher's coat.

She looked around the house. She could do a lot more before heading home if Will took Asher. "That would be great, thanks, Will."

That stretching feeling in her chest grew again as she gave her brother a hug. She didn't know what had gotten into him lately, but she liked it.

And then, suddenly everyone was gone.

Leaving Stephanie and Julian alone.

"Are you sure you don't want some help?" she asked, looking at the mess left behind. There were lobster shells piled up, melted butter stuck to everything, and dirty bibs and utensils scattered everywhere. "Seriously, it'll help me get to know the kitchen."

Julian took a minute before answering. "Sure. I'll start with the dishes."

"Okay," she said. With the little time she had been here, she had learned a few spots, like where they kept their linens. She opened the drawer and pulled out a drying cloth. The material felt so soft against her hands. The rich even had beautiful dish towels. "Are these from that little fabric shop downtown?"

"Yeah," he said. "Muriel's sister owns it."

Things suddenly started clicking together in her head like a lock being undone. All the small connections between the family. "Isn't there a woman named Bonnie who's involved? She runs the factory out by the river."

"LeCroix Fabrics," he said. "I think that's Cora's supplier. Cora owns Blueberry Bay Linens. All our linens are hers."

Stephanie remembered reading the name Blueberry Bay Linens in the binder. "Muriel's sister?"

"Yes, she's really…nice." Julian took a dish towel and held it in his hands. "You two would get along great."

"Really?" Stephanie didn't think he knew her well enough to find a friend she'd get along *great* with. "I doubt it. Most people here don't want to hang out with someone whose curfew is seventy thirty."

Julian looked at the clock. "It's almost nine, and you're still here."

She grabbed a large pot and started drying it. "Money trumps everything."

She pointed to the walk-in pantry for the pots and pans she had found.

"Yup, it goes in there," Julian said.

Everything in the Abbotts' culinary-dream kitchen had its place, an exquisite order created from years of high-quality chefs working in the house and Janet's keen sense of detail.

"This place has everything," she said from the pantry, noticing all the different-sized pots and pans—copper, stainless steel, and cast iron—all hanging or resting perfectly in a way that looked, well… beautiful.

"It's definitely well stocked." Julian came walking in with a couple more pans.

"Dinner was really good." Stephanie didn't want to sound like she was kissing up to the boss, but she had been impressed. "That sauce! I'll need the recipe."

"It's in the—"

"Binder," she finished for him, shaking her pointer finger.

He placed the pan down. "You're doing a good job."

"You mean in the few days I've walked behind Janet?" She knew he was just being kind. "It's been nice, but I still have a lot to learn."

He nodded and pointed to a large empty spot perfect for a lobster pot.

"Do you think your grandfather will like me?" she asked nervously.

"He's going to love you."

# CHAPTER 12

There had not been one morning that Stephanie hadn't had to drag Asher out of bed, most of the time with tears, sometimes a fight, but constantly breaking Stephanie's heart. But today, it was a completely different story. After she'd gotten home from Julian's, Will had told her that Muriel had called to let them know that she talked to Colin's mother and that the bus buddy was a go. Asher had been so excited that he'd snuck out of his bedroom to talk to her about it last night.

Now, he was up before she had even reached his room.

"Morning," he said, scrambling past her.

"Morning..." She turned to watch her little man walk past her in clean clothes. "Are you already dressed? You know you don't have school today, right?"

"I know." Asher said heading to the kitchen. "Uncle Will said I had to help with breakfast before we go out on the boat," Asher said.

She groaned about Will passing off breakfast, the one chore he was in charge of, but when she got into the kitchen, Will was standing with Asher, teaching him how to crack an egg. And it was nice.

"Hey," she said to her older brother. At first, she tiptoed

around, worried she'd gotten the situation wrong and Asher was in the way.

"Do you see this?" Will said to Stephanie as Asher cracked an egg. "I think we may have a chef in the family."

A piece of the shell fell into the yolk.

"That's okay, little dude. Let's just pluck it out of there," Will said, winking at Asher. "Get it? Pluck? Like a chicken?"

"Huh?" Asher's eyebrows wrinkled in confusion.

"Never mind," Will said. He looked up to Stephanie. "Eggs?"

"Sure." Stephanie didn't know what had changed in Will, but she liked it. She couldn't remember the last time he had included her in his mandatory breakfast chore. He thought he didn't have to make meals since he fished for lobsters all day. She wished he wasn't being utterly sexist about it, but her brother had just expected her to do it for no reason other than that she was a woman. He also considered fishing all day work, whereas waiting tables all day was like hanging out with friends.

"You know, I think this new job of yours is going to be great," Will said from the stove. He handed Asher a whisk. "Now you get to scramble the eggs by carefully whipping the whisk."

Will first took the whisk between both hands and whipped it back and forth, then let Asher take over.

"Now you think it's a good idea?" *How things have changed.* "Well, good, because it's my job."

"Julian seems good," Will said.

She noticed Will looked good too. His eyes were bright and clear. He wasn't groggy or irritated.

"You seem like you got a good night's sleep," she said, pouring herself a cup of coffee.

Will looked up from the stove. "You know, I slept better last night than I have in a long time."

She so badly wanted to point out that he hadn't drank last night, but she wouldn't be the nag who pointed out annoying things. If Will wanted to slow down or quit drinking, that would have to be up to him. He wasn't going to change his mind just because she said so. She knew better. Look at her marriage with Gabe. He'd found her to be a nag when she pointed out how much he had been drinking, and he used it as an excuse as to why he'd left the marriage to sleep with other women.

"That's great," she said, milling behind them and making sure no one burned down the house.

"I think I'm going to start running with Julian after work," Will said.

"Really?" Now, things have just become insane. "You haven't gotten off the couch since your senior football season." She tried to do the math in her head. "Asher, how long has that been?"

"Don't do the math." Will held up a spatula to Asher's mouth. "Julian mentioned that nights are hard being alone. I need to get in shape, and he likes to run, so..." Will shrugged as he returned to the eggs. "It was nice to hang out with him again."

She smiled at that. "Yeah, it was."

"He's the same, in a way," Will said.

"Uncle Will, they're starting to do something," Asher said from the stove.

Will's attention was diverted to the eggs, and then, as if the day of surprises couldn't get even more unexpected, he said, "Why don't you take your shower now, and I'll have breakfast waiting when you're done."

She didn't even stop to say thank you. She kissed them both on the cheek and rushed off to the open bathroom. She never got a shower first.

When she returned to the kitchen, all the boys, including her father, had sat down for breakfast. Asher had them saying a prayer before the meal, which melted her heart. Will even had his phone down. When she joined them, she could almost feel her mother's presence. She could feel her over her shoulder, watching everyone eat, ensuring they had enough, and rushing around the kitchen to get more.

"Gram would be so proud of you," she said to Asher, but she

could've also said it to Will. "She said if you can cook scrambled eggs, you can cook anything."

Asher beamed at the table. "Julian said that real men cook."

That made her laugh. "Is that why you have a sudden interest?"

Will ruffled Asher's hair, messing it up. "You should go brush your teeth."

"I will," Asher said, picking up his plate.

"And brush that mop of hair of yours," Will teased.

Asher's mouth dropped. "You messed it up."

"Your pillow messed it up." Will got up and picked up his plate. "Let's finish cleaning up the kitchen."

Stephanie didn't know what had gotten into her brother. Maybe it was hanging out with Julian. Maybe it was the Christmas spirit. Or maybe he'd just realized that he needed to step up his game at this point in his life. Whatever it was, Stephanie was all for it.

"So, I'm just going to head to the diner then," she said, backing toward the door.

"See you later," her dad said from the newspaper.

"Bye, Mommy!" Asher said from the sink.

Will waved with the dish wand in his hand. "Have a good day."

"Okay." She stood there watching the scene.

"Bye," she said, but no one heard her with the water running and the coffee pot brewing.

Stephanie even arrived at the diner early. "Hey, Lindy."

"Hey, girl," Lindy said in her thick Down East accent. "You're wicked early."

"I know." Stephanie put her purse in the small locker Lindy provided the wait staff. "Asher was all set."

"He had a good morning?" Lindy asked, knowing the difficulties Stephanie had been having.

"Yeah. He just changed, like, literally overnight." Stephanie knew Muriel's arrangement with his buddy had everything to do with it, but the change still felt so sudden and abrupt. She didn't want to say she missed the clinging, sad Asher, but the idea he could grow up that quickly scared her. She might miss other stages she did love. What was the saying? The days were long, but the years were short.

"Well, that's great," Lindy said. "Makes going to work a little easier on moms."

Stephanie had enjoyed her walk to work that morning. A light dusting of snow covered the surface of everything outside, muting the streetlights' glow just a smidge. The magic of Christmas was displayed through the town's lights, decorations, and garland. Everything sounded quieter except the mighty Atlantic's pounding waves in the background.

She didn't spend any time worrying about Asher. She didn't think about him at all. Someone else took over her thoughts.

Julian Abbott.

Things had gotten exponentially better since he'd stepped back into her life. Maybe everything just happened for a reason and it really had nothing to do with Julian but, instead, it was just timing and fate?

But it certainly felt like Julian had a part in it.

She could feel all those old, crazy teenage feelings filling her up and making her feel completely out of control.

Even at work, she saw things that reminded her of Julian, like the woman sitting in the booth who looked like Janet.

Stephanie did a double take. Was that Janet?

She walked to the older woman sitting alone in the booth in Stephanie's section. "Janet?"

Janet turned around as Stephanie came to the table. She smiled. "Good, you're early."

Stephanie looked at her watch. She had a half hour before her shift.

"I thought we could go over a few things while I have breakfast," Janet said.

"I'm at work," Stephanie said.

"It's fine." Janet looked past Stephanie to the breakfast bar where Lindy stood and waved at her. "I talked to Lindy, and she said she's fine with it."

But Stephanie didn't feel that was right, whether Lindy said it was fine or not. "Lindy's paying me for my time. I'm sorry, Janet. I can't work until tonight."

Janet tapped the tablet she had opened to a spreadsheet. "I'll be quick."

But she wasn't quick, and she spent the morning going over all the different steps she had to take before leaving for the night.

"I realize this is very rushed, but Mr. Abbott likes everything ready for when he wakes up," Janet said.

That meant his breakfast bowl, plate, silverware, and linen napkin were laid out on the breakfast tray the night before, with his coffee mug and a glass for juice. All his medication lined up in alphabetical order, and a spot for the morning *Boston Globe*.

"We'll talk meal prep and ordering groceries tonight," Janet said as Stephanie dropped a plate of pancakes onto the table. Janet looked around the diner. "Did you do the decorating for the holidays?"

Lindy had draped the whole diner with tinsel garland and green and red colored lights. A large vintage Santa Claus stood in the corner, and every table had its own tiny plastic Christmas tree that lit up.

Stephanie shook her head, about to say how she loved the way Lindy took old Blueberry Bay remnants and repurposed them into ornaments, but Janet said, "Good. This is a bit tacky, if you ask me."

Stephanie liked Janet, but she had a deep loyalty to Lindy. She didn't want to botch this job at the get-go, but she couldn't come into her place of work for over a decade and speak ill of it. This had been her refuge when parenting got hard. Lindy had been there for her in more ways than she could explain. Being a single mother herself, Lindy understood the challenges of raising a kid alone.

"Lindy seems to know what the customers want, because they love the vibe," she said, hoping the negativity might stop.

Janet closed her eyes as she took her first bite. "I forgot how good the food is here."

"Why don't I bring some pie tonight?" Stephanie said, handing her the receipt.

Janet mumbled a yes as she took another bite of pancake. She held up the fork at Stephanie, then swallowed before saying, "You should peek inside the linen shop down by the park, Blueberry Bay Linens. You should get to know the people you'll be dealing with."

Janet may be a bit bossy for Stephanie and a little over the top about the darn binders, but she hadn't stayed a house manager for thirty-plus years for a family like the Abbotts without knowing a thing or two. She was an ace at her job, and if that meant being confident and direct and over the top about memorizing every word in the darn binders, then she would do it.

And Stephanie knew how to ace things too.

# CHAPTER 13

When Will texted Julian and joked about being a sternman again, Julian didn't hesitate at another chance at being out on the water. But the problem was, his father had set up a meeting with his old boss to talk about the possibilities of coming back to the company. But he couldn't pass up the opportunity to go out on the water, even if his dad had pulled a lot of strings.

But it was worth it. Being out on the water, even in December, had been just as magical as it had been when he was a kid. The open Atlantic, the fresh air, and the excitement of what they were about to uncover by dragging up the lobster pots from the deep blue sea. He spent the day with Will and Will's sternman, Greg.

"Greg's purchasing his own boat," Will said as they drove back to the harbor. "I'm going to have to find another sternman to fill his spot."

"Will it be difficult?" Julian asked.

Will shrugged. "There's a lot of people who want to be sponsored."

"You have to be sponsored to become a lobsterman?" Julian had no idea. He just thought you had to get a fishing license.

"It's a two-year stint," Will explained. "And it doesn't pay much."

Julian's phone rang in his pocket for the dozenth time. He didn't even have to look to know it was his father calling about why he canceled his appointment with the company. He ignored his phone as Will docked the boat.

*Ah, the company*, Julian thought to himself as he left Will and Asher at the docks. How could he return to the city when he could be on the water all day?

He had asked, half-jokingly, how hard it was to become a lobster fisherman. He thought Will's excitement was a joke as well, but when Will opened up the application to get a sternman license on his phone and offered to sponsor him, he had to let him down.

"My dad wants me back at the company," Julian said. "But I'd much rather be out here fishing all day."

Diversified Business and Credit was his father's dream career for Julian. But now, after rehab and this past year sober, it felt like a joke. All the schmoozing and boozing with clients made his stomach turn. The way he'd tried to impress the higher executives embarrassed him. The fancy conferences he'd attended at luxury resorts seemed wasteful. The company sedan he loved now felt impractical in Maine. The nights in the city—all expenses paid—now felt like a distant memory. He didn't care about the courtside tickets now. What good was going to a game when he had no one to go with?

"All you need is a sponsor to start the process," Will said. "Though, I'm not sure how long this girl will make it," he added, as he slapped the side of the boat.

"Will you be able to buy a new one?" Julian asked.

"Maybe." Will shrugged. "But without a sternman, I won't be able to haul enough to earn enough."

Julian knew Will's lobster boat had been his father's when they were kids and had seen better days. Every summer, when he could convince Will to bring him along, he'd go out with Will and his dad to catch the gold of the sea. It had been some of his best memories. He could never look at the Atlantic Ocean without thinking about being on that boat.

Julian passed by the local toy shop as he drove down Main Street. Every Christmas, he'd drag his mother to look at the new toys on display, praying Santa would find him in Maine. Not unsurprisingly, he seemed to come every year without fail. He smiled at the thought as he pulled over and shut the car off.

He decided to go inside and look at what's new, maybe even get a new Transformer for Asher. He'd have to get the little guy something good. After Will had told him about Asher's dad, he wanted to buy the whole toy store for the kid. How could a father walk away from his son? It was mind-blowing that Gabe chose to ruin his marriage, but to desert his son? He had to be insane.

He'd never interacted with Gabe beyond an occasional run-in at the bars here and there, but he knew he didn't like him.

The afternoon sun had long since fallen behind the trees, and the streetlights had come on. Light snowflakes began falling, and Julian could feel his younger self getting excited as he approached the lit-up storefront of Yankee Toy Store. He pressed the brass latch and opened the door. The tiny toy store was just as he remembered.

"Welcome back!" Mr. Zhang said to Julian as the bell rang against the door's glass.

Julian wondered if he remembered him or if that's what he said to all his customers.

"Are you looking for anything in particular?" the store owner asked.

Julian hummed an "Umm," as he thought of his answer. Would it be weird if he bought Christmas presents for Asher? Should he ask Stephanie first? Maybe she wanted to get him a new Transformer from Santa, and he would ruin things. "I'm just browsing for now."

"Well, if you decide to check out the Transformers, I've moved that section to the back," Mr. Zhang said. "Not as popular as when you were a kid."

Julian let out a laugh. "You still remember me after all these years?"

"You're a hard one to forget." Mr. Zhang let out a laugh of his own. "You spent all summer coming in and checking out my selection."

"That's because it took me all summer to buy that Optimus Prime."

"Everyone always thought you kids were spoiled," Mr. Zhang said.

Julian didn't know what people thought of them.

"But I used to tell everyone about how you would work for your toys." The store owner shook his head. "Your father taught you how to respect a dollar."

Julian didn't see it as respecting money as much as making him fear not having it.

If he didn't do well in school, get good grades, and get a good education, his father would tell him he'd end up like Mr. Zhang, working hard for the rest of his life to earn barely enough to get by.

His father would use people like Mr. Zhang and Janet as examples of how not to live and encourage him to continue in their banking and finance family business even though Julian never had any interest in it.

"They work their tails off, and for what?" his father would say from his fancy foreign car, yacht, or high-rise office building.

Maybe they and all the other countless workers had it hard, but they also had the freedom he'd never felt while working in finance. They didn't hide behind their title. They were honest and living their best lives with what they had. They looked out for others and didn't take from their neighbors. They gave their service with kindness and grace.

He couldn't say the same for the people he had worked with for almost ten years.

All people did at his company was take, take, and take some more. They took their clients' money, employees' time, and wrecked their mental and physical well-being by running their workers day and night. Honesty wasn't a policy people in his company strived for; if anything, most people were shady with their integrity, and he never trusted anyone, not even his dad.

"I'm looking for the newest Transformer, actually," he told Mr. Zhang. "You're Bryce, right?"

Mr. Zhang nodded. "We don't have the newest one here today, but I'd happily order it for you."

Julian hesitated for only a second before saying yes. "Will you call me as soon as you get it in?"

"Sure will," Mr. Zhang said as he typed into a computer. "It's going to be here first thing tomorrow."

"That quick?" He remembered having to wait weeks when he was a kid. Or was it because he was a kid, and it only felt like weeks? "It's amazing how fast things can be delivered these days," Julian said, trying to continue with the small talk. Something about the fact that the man still remembered him as the little boy who had saved up his money to buy a toy felt good.

"Too bad people can't even wait a day," Bryce said. "These days, people come in, see what they want, and order it online."

"Right in front of you?" Julian felt sorry for the store owner.

He nodded. "Right on their phones there's an app to find the item they're looking for. Small shops like mine are barely surviving. We can't keep up with the big places."

What a shame that this man who remembered the names of his customers and what their niche toy had been years later couldn't keep up with commercial giants.

"Do you mind keeping an account for me?" Julian said. "I may want to come back and order more."

Bryce nodded quickly. "Of course."

"And I'd like to purchase a few gifts for the community toy drive," Julian said, pointing at a large bin where toys had been donated. "Do you know if they need any help?"

"The Queen Bees?" Bryce shook his head. "They usually have everything under control by now. Most of the donations come from the festival over the summer."

Julian didn't know what the Queen Bees were or what they did. He remembered a festival but didn't know when or what kind of festival it was. He wondered if they sold honey.

"I'd like to donate at least five toys for the bin," Julian said, pulling out his credit card.

"Why don't you pick them out for the kids?" Bryce held out his hand towards the many shelves packed full of toys.

Before Julian knew it, he'd walked up and down each aisle, picking out many toys for the kids in Blueberry Bay. He picked out GI Joes, Barbies, LEGO sets, and many more. He felt like a kid again, seeing all the new designs and updated versions of the toys he'd had when he was younger. After filling a cart, he paid Bryce.

"I'll call you when the Transformer comes in," Bruce said as Julian began to leave.

"That's great, thanks," Julian said, thinking about how the kids who may not have had a gift under the tree now wouldn't have to feel let down. As cheesy as it sounded, it felt good to give. He wasn't entirely sure if he had ever donated like that. Yes, he had donated, but only when confronted with having to do so. He never just did it on his own because he wanted to help. Why didn't he want to help more?

He had been taught to hoard his money and keep it close to his belt, which meant it was safe and within the family. He had been taught to only worry about the Abbott family because no one else mattered.

The LaBelle family had barely had enough and had always given to others. They'd given their time and energy to Julian just like they had to their own children. They'd fed him, even though the Abbotts never repaid the favor. They'd let him sleep over every night if that's what Will and Julian had wanted. They'd never asked for anything in return.

When Mr. LaBelle's boat had been damaged by an unexpected storm, it had devastated him. He had to get extra jobs around town to make ends meet. Mrs. LaBelle had started working at the diner. That's when Will had to get a job as a sternman with one of his uncles. Their summers of freedom and goofing off together had abruptly ended, and Julian had thought it was unfair. Surely, the Abbotts could have spared a little of their wealth to help his second family?

"We didn't get where we are by being a charity," his father had said when Julian had told him their story.

"But he can't fish," Julian had protested. "They just need to fix the boat. Will said they could lose their house."

"A fisherman should know enough to save in case of things like that." Steven Abbott had put his hands on Julian's shoulders and looked down into his eyes. "There are people who bust their butt and those who want something for nothing." Steven Abbott wouldn't even consider the fact that they had probably already spent thousands on his son without even a hesitation.

He'd never asked for money again. He hadn't wanted to go to a fancy prep school and an Ivy League college. He felt embarrassed driving luxury vehicles he couldn't afford without his daddy. He never wanted the money he had been given when he'd turned twenty-one through a trust set up by his great-grandfather. He hadn't even expected to get anything in his grandmother's will.

He could use it for charity now, he supposed.

"Would you let me know if you need more donations?" Julian asked Bryce. "I'd hate for any family to go without during the holiday season."

The store owner grinned. "That's generous of you, Jules."

Julian smiled at the name. "Anything I can do to help, let me know."

Bryce gave him a nod and said goodbye.

For the rest of the afternoon, Julian wished he had taken Will's offer to go over there for dinner but he felt like having dinner with them three nights in a row would be pushing it. He was technically Stephanie's boss. She might not want him around all the time. Plus, being around her did something to him that he couldn't deny, and the more time he spent with her, the more he felt that feeling, and the more time he wanted to spend with her.

When he got to his house, he almost missed all the candles twinkling in the windows, his mind racing about new things he could do for the community.

"You're finally home," Janet said.

"Yeah?" He hadn't missed a meeting with Stephanie, had he? "Was I supposed to be home?"

"You're not usually gone all day, that's all." Janet put her hands on her hips. "It's nice to see you go out with Will again."

He felt the same. "It's nice to reconnect with the LaBelles. They're a great family."

Janet nodded. "Yes, the salt of the earth."

"I wanted to get Christmas presents for Asher and Stephanie and the rest of the family," he said, mostly thinking out loud. He'd felt so good giving to the toy drive that he didn't want to stop. "And you too, Janet. I want to give you and Billy something for your new adventure."

Janet let out a holler of a laugh. "What has gotten into you?"

"What do you mean?"

She shook her head. "Don't go and break that girl's heart. She's gone through enough with that jerk of an ex-husband."

"Excuse me?" Had he missed something?

"I can tell you like her." Janet shook her finger at him when he started denying it. "It's written all over your face. You can't even look at me when you deny it."

It was true. He had looked away. "So. What if I do like her? She's incredible."

Janet's smile fell. "She has been hurt enough."

Even after a year of sobriety, a stay in a rehabilitation center, and no women for over a year, for goodness' sake, Janet still didn't see the change. And she was the only person over the past year who had seen him daily.

"You're right," he said, feeling defeated. "I should keep my distance."

"It's not just a job, but her livelihood," Janet said, continuing to make perfect sense. "Her family depends on her working."

As much as it hurt, he couldn't deny that Janet was right. Someone like Julian would only hurt her, because he hadn't changed. He wasn't this new person who cared about others, cared for his neighbors, or even respected others more than himself.

He should stay away from Stephanie.

# CHAPTER 14

*S*tephanie hadn't worked at the Abbott house much during the day, always coming over after her shifts at the diner and getting there after dark. So, today she looked forward to seeing the house in the sunlight.

It had been two days since she had last been there, and the more she went to the Abbott house, the more overwhelmed she felt by the scope of being the family's house manager. And she hadn't even met Julian's grandfather, the patriarch of the Abbott Dynasty. She had heard a mixed bag from everyone at the diner who had heard of her new endeavor.

Some said Max Abbott was a cold man. He rarely mixed with the locals. Even though he had been coming to Blueberry Bay his whole life, he stayed to himself. He didn't attend any of the events in Blueberry Bay, didn't shop in the local stores, and never seemed to be out and about outside of his own residence.

Muriel had been the only person besides Julian with a kind thing to say about him. Even Janet seemed intimidated by her boss. Even more so when Steven, Julian's father, was mentioned.

She pulled onto the fresh snow on the driveway and slowly drove to the back of the house, where she was to park. She went through her to-do list in her head for the dozenth time. There was so much to do, and those binders were intense, filled with instructions and lists. It was too much, from home appliance instructions, like how to use the washing machine, to special directions on hand-washing the passed-down linens in the fifth drawer in the china cabinet in the pantry.

"We need to order wreaths and garland!" Janet exclaimed as soon as Stephanie walked in the door.

Stephanie had to register Janet's panic for a second. She slowly shook her head. She had read through the binders. "I saw nothing about ordering fresh wreaths and garland. It said there were artificial wreaths and garland in the barn."

"They're ruined!" Janet looked like she might hyperventilate. "Someone moved things around and left some of the containers open. Mice got inside and must have lived there for years." Janet let out a huff.

"I'm sure we can find garland," Stephanie said, but Janet was already complaining.

"It's too late now," Janet continued. "The trees are going to be delivered today." She threw up her hands. "We'll have to make do."

"We could go out and make some," Julian said from behind.

Stephanie did a full jump in surprise. She hadn't heard him come in. "Wow. Where did you sneak up from?"

"Sorry, I just heard something about not ordering garland." Julian stood in the doorway to what would be Stephanie's office. He leaned against its frame, tucking his hands in his perfect-fit jeans. "I could collect some pine branches and stuff from the woods."

Stephanie shook her head to stop checking him out. "No, let me do it. I can go to the woods behind my house. I can even get Asher to help."

Janet looked at her watch. "The trees will be delivered in a few hours. We still need to set everything up beforehand."

Stephanie knew that what seemed like a simple problem could be another person's crisis, so she tried not to judge Janet's irrationality or allow this to add to her own anxiety about meeting this man who Janet was losing her mind over.

"It's okay, Janet," Julian said in a calming voice. He walked over to her and placed his hand on her shoulder. "He's going to be fine as long as he has his whiskey and cigar."

Janet's eyes widened. "He didn't tell you?"

"Tell me what?" Julian asked.

"Your parents are coming." Janet looked like she had just told him an apocalypse was about to begin.

And Julian's reaction would be one she'd never forget. He was hurt.

"Oh," he said. "No, they didn't tell me."

Janet started telling Julian about her long conversation with his mother. How they were flying from New York to Boston, then up to Maine for a few days, and after they were to fly off to Paris to see his mother's family.

"Will you be going with your parents?" Stephanie asked, more curious for herself than for her role as house manager.

"No." He shook his head. "I wasn't asked to go."

He glanced at Janet and Stephanie briefly and then gave them a hard nod before walking out of Janet's office. "I'm going to get the garland."

"Where?" Janet asked as he left the room.

"Outside." he said. "There's plenty around here."

"Julian, wait." Stephanie ran after him.

By the time she caught up to him, he had made it through the kitchen and into the dining room.

"I'll help with the garland," she said, hoping the pain she saw in his eyes may have been a mistake.

But she could see the hurt so clearly as he turned to face her. His emotions were written across his face. How could his parents not include him in their plans for Christmas?

"I promised Janet I'd help you with the house manager position," he said as soon as he turned around. "But do you think you'd be okay if I went back to the city?"

Suddenly, Janet's panic transferred to her. "Wait, what? You're leaving?"

She thought about meeting Steven Abbott and how awkward it would be. The town had a very unfavorable opinion of Steven Abbott. They may not know the elder recluse Max Abbott, which made them suspicious. But no one liked Steven Abbott, and everyone in town had warned her plenty about him. Now, his son didn't want to stay for the holidays when he was coming around.

"You don't want to spend the holidays here?" It didn't make sense to her. The whole binder talked about the "Family Christmas." Each member of the Abbott family had a tab listing all the Christmas presents Corrine Abbott, aka Mrs. Claus, had delivered on Christmas Eve. She even had photocopied Christmas lists and a "Likes and Interests" page.

"Your grandmother would be heartbroken." She had spent all that time and energy documenting how she did things so nothing would change. "She wanted you all to keep having Christmas together."

"Well, she doesn't know what Christmas is like now," Julian said harshly.

And that pain in his eyes seemed to get deeper.

"Oh, sorry." She retreated a step back. "I shouldn't have said that."

It was out of line and none of her business. How dare she make him feel guilty for not wanting to spend time with people who didn't even have the decency to call and tell him their plans. And if she was truly being honest, it was her own insecurities that were bothering her.

"I'm sorry," he said back to her. "I shouldn't have snapped. My father and I don't have a relationship like you and your family."

She let out a laugh. "You're kidding, right?"

He looked at her, wrinkling his brow.

"We're not like the Partridge family." She laughed at the idea. "Half the time, I want to kill Will. He's usually at the bar or hanging out with friends. And my dad, well, he just hasn't been the same since my mom died."

There wasn't more she could say about him. He tried his best, but the person who made their house a home had been her mother. She tried to fill her shoes, but they were tight and perfect, and she just didn't fit.

She shrugged. "I'm just nervous to meet your family."

He tilted his head. "You? Nervous? You always seem like you're in control."

"Well, I should've gone to acting school, because I don't know what I'm doing most of the time." Her in control? Now, that was funny. Her whole life felt like it was spiraling out of control.

And it was as if God had to prove a point. Her phone rang, and Gabe's name flashed across the screen. She silenced it, but her mood instantly changed.

"You okay?" he asked.

She nodded, and lied, "Yeah, I'm fine."

He furrowed his brows at that.

"I am," she said, but he kept giving her that look. "I'm going to get some garland and hit the beach."

"The beach?" he asked.

"Yeah, for the garland," she answered. "For good luck." Then it hit her. She hadn't read anything in the binder about the long-standing tradition in Blueberry Bay to decorate using shells from the sea.

She walked back to the kitchen and grabbed her coat, then stuffed her hands into gloves and put on a hat and scarf.

"Is that why you had so many shells on your tree?" he asked.

"Yes." She zipped up her coat, looking at him. "You haven't heard of this tradition?"

She couldn't believe it.

"It's what Hallmark movies are made of." She would have thought after all these years of coming to Blueberry Bay, he'd be aware of this tradition. "It started with the first town celebration. They put up a tree in the town square, and all the schoolchildren made a shell ornament. It's gotten bigger over the years. Now there are vendors, and the town serves hot cocoa for everyone. There are even carolers and a horse-drawn carriage ride. Santa comes in on a boat to greet all the children and give gifts to everyone. But at the night's end, the kids keep the ornament for their family's tree. That's why we have so many. Two kids, twelve years in school, and now I have Asher."

She thought about how lucky she was to live in such a special place.

"I never went to school here. That's probably why I've never heard of it," Julian said.

"Oh, yeah." Stephanie wondered if he thought the whole thing sounded corny. From what she had read in the binder, a free cup of hot cocoa was nothing compared to their family traditions. "That's why there's so many shells as decorations around town."

He thought about it for a moment. "I guess I hadn't paid attention."

"I know it probably sounds pretty lame, but it's what we do around these parts for entertainment."

He shook his head. "I think it sounds nice."

She smiled at that. Her eyes sprang open as she remembered it was that upcoming weekend.

"You should come with us. I mean, if you want to. It's in a couple of days, but you should come. You'll love it."

He shook his head. "I think it's time for me to return to the city."

They both stepped out the back door. Julian was dressed like he was walking down Commonwealth Avenue, not the Maine Atlantic coast.

"You're going to freeze."

"You sound like Janet," he said.

She expected him to say *mother* in that phrase, not Janet. She wasn't sure if he would talk about things, but he seemed happy in Blueberry Bay. "If you can't stay at the house because you and your parents don't get along, you should stay with us until they leave. Or is there more to the story?"

She wasn't sure if she was crossing the line now, but if he left because of these people, maybe she didn't want to work for them.

"I mean, do I want to work for your family?" She thought about what he had told her when she'd first had the interview, how Janet didn't want to hire her because his parents would probably sell the house if Max Abbott were to pass away.

He took a deep breath and exhaled slowly. "It's that I don't want to work for *him*."

"Oh." She didn't even know that he worked for his father. She realized she didn't even know what Julian did. She just thought he did what rich people did, whatever that was.

"My father just saw this path for me, and I couldn't hack it." He shrugged.

"That's okay," she said. "It's not your path."

"Tell that to Steven Abbott." He mumbled something under his breath, then stopped walking. "Where are we going?"

She pointed down the driveway and started walking again. "We're headed to the beach first."

She went to the back of the house and down the walkway toward the water. A blanket of freshly fallen snow covered the gardens. She had loved playing among the beach rosebushes and perfectly trimmed hedges along the water. Like she'd come across a real-life secret garden just a path away.

She'd have to ask Janet if she should tell the landscapers to put lights out there. It must look like a winter wonderland. She could only imagine what it would look like all lit up.

That's when she noticed the statue.

"Is that a Jacob O'Neill?" She trekked through the snow in her boots to the bronze statue and brushed off the snow covering her face.

"It's a mer—"

"Mermaid," she finished for him. She stared at the woman's face. "It's not the same."

"It's actually the same mermaid, just her younger self," he said, pointing to her face. "It's Jacob's wife when she was younger."

"Did you know him?" she had heard about the hermit artist her whole life.

"He taught my brother and me how to surf."

Jacob O'Neill had been sort of a legend before he'd died. She had never seen him but had run through his yard hundreds of times to get to the beach. She never knew that the hermit artist had been world-renowned for his artwork. She knew him because he had survived the most tragic shipwreck in Blueberry Bay history. Her father still couldn't mention it without tearing up, having lost an uncle and two friends in the storm of the century.

She frowned.

"What's wrong?" he asked, looking around.

"I can't believe this is your backyard!" She held out her arms at the view. She could see everything from that spot. The town at the center of the harbor. Her speckle of a house across the bay. The lighthouse perched on the island in the middle of the ocean. How could he leave this for a crowded, dirty city? "Seriously, don't leave because of your dad."

He looked out at the view. "I don't want to, but I need to."

She could tell he was holding back. How could she blame him? He shouldn't trust a stranger with his feelings.

"He thinks I'm a loser," he said, kicking a small piece of ice off the walkway into the snow.

"I doubt your dad thinks you're a loser," she said, but she could hear how patronizing that sounded. "Ugh, I sound like *my father*." She dropped her arms, slapping her sides with them. "I bet my father thinks I'm a bit of a loser, too."

Julian shot a look of disbelief at her.

"I was supposed to be the one who went to college," she said, keeping her eyes on the horizon, praying her emotions wouldn't get the best of her. "I was so good at school that everyone thought I'd end up somewhere or doing something big. Even I

131

thought I would become this high-powered attorney who comes back to town and is asked to speak about how I made it. Now the only speech I'll ever be asked to give is about using contraception."

Julian turned to her, staring into her eyes as if he were looking into her soul. "If you ask me, Asher's that something special you did."

Her mouth dropped as her heart swelled with feelings. She wasn't sure if she had ever felt this way before. She bit her lip, then said, "That's the nicest thing anyone has ever said to me."

And for a moment, they just stared at each other. Their eyes locked in, and she swore for a second that he might come in to kiss her, but instead, he jolted back, his eyes on the water. "We should get those shells."

She tried to steady her breathing, but her heart raced out of control. Should she whip her arms around his neck and pull him into her? What did she have to lose at this point?

Unless, of course, she had totally read the signals wrong. She thought back to the last part of their conversation. He had mentioned not wanting to work with his father, not exactly a topic that created a romantic atmosphere. Making out after sharing that he felt like a loser might be the wrong time.

"You're not a loser," she said. "And your father's stupid for saying such a thing about his son. I'd be proud if Asher grew up to be a man with as much integrity and kindness as you."

Julian stuffed his hands into his coat pockets. "I think it's just easy to be myself around you."

Before she could think better of it, she just acted. She reached out for his hand and pulled it out of his pocket to hold in hers. And they stood there, looking out at the water. It wasn't a kiss, but as he squeezed it back, she knew something had happened between them. Something magical and wonderful.

# CHAPTER 15

$\mathcal{J}$ulian took Stephanie to his grandfather's beach, where they collected shells. The sandy beach hadn't been cleaned up in months and had accumulated enough seashells for the whole town to decorate a tree. They collected sea glass and driftwood. They didn't hold hands again, but Julian could still feel his fingers tingle from her touch.

Emotions swelled inside him each time he thought of their fingers intertwined. After she had let go, he'd wanted her hand back in his.

"Did you ever attend the Christmas ball?" Stephanie asked as they filled the last bag with one more sand dollar. The snow along the edge of the beach crunched under her feet.

Julian had never heard of it. "My grandparents had a ball?"

She nodded her head. "Yeah, it was a big deal. There was an article in *The Boston Globe* about it," she said. "Janet showed me the newspaper clipping."

"Here at the house?" Julian didn't even remember hearing about it.

"In the front hall," she said, heading toward the stairs that brought them up to the house.

Julian had been to plenty of parties at the summer house, but never at Christmas. He pictured a string quartet playing Christmas songs that could be heard as soon as the guests arrived. The Christmas tree in the middle of the spiral staircase would steal everyone's attention when they walked through the door. The fireplace would be aglow with amber flames. Guests would mingle among little boy and girl carolers with hot chocolate or eggnog in their hands. Servers would float around the room with silver trays filled with Christmas delicacies and drinks. Alcoholic drinks.

Julian would have to confront the possibility that when his father and mother showed up, there would be a lot of booze. His grandfather had been more than supportive of his sobriety. He hadn't balked at getting rid of the stuff in the house and locking the wine cellar until further notice.

But his parents were a different story. His father especially loved his drinks. He would never give it up for Julian, especially during the holidays, which showed the problem right there. They weren't going to sacrifice for each other. Julian wasn't willing to lose his soul for a company that didn't care about him, and his father wasn't going to lose his only friend—the one thing that never let him down—alcohol.

"I'm afraid I'll drink," he said, so quietly the waves almost covered his words, which he wished were the case as soon as he'd said it. Should he open up to her? Should he share his most intimate secrets with her and risk her changing her feelings? Or should he hide things and let it blow up in his face like all his other relationships? "It's been over a year since I had a drink."

His addiction had been an hour-to-hour thing by the time he'd gotten help. Now, he had days when he didn't want to grab the bottle. But that might change when his parents arrived.

Stephanie frowned. "How do you get through the days now?"

He shrugged. "Hide, mostly."

"You can't live your life hiding." She grabbed hold of his hand and held on to it. "But you can get through it. I promise. And if you need a little extra support, you have me and Will and my dad…and Asher."

"It means a lot that you are saying that." And he meant it, too. He had to remember that people were in his corner. He just needed to get out of his head long enough to notice.

"Do you ever just wish you could start over?" he asked.

"I've always wanted to finish actually," she said, looking out at the water. "I never got to complete college. I had dreamt of becoming a doctor. When I got pregnant, I was just expected to give up my dreams and take care of the baby. Not that I regret a thing, because I love being a mom, but I wouldn't want to start over, just finish."

After the beach, they headed to the back woods on his grandfather's property to collect whatever they could find for the garland. Stephanie collected branches of white pine and hemlocks. She found small clusters of greenery with tiny bright red berries. She collected pinecones and twigs.

"I know your grandmother had a ton of ribbons and things in her sewing room," Stephanie said.

Her phone buzzed again, and she checked it, then silenced it.

"You can take the call," he said.

She shook her head. "No, I don't want to."

He could feel her hesitating but didn't want to push it. She had been patient with him, and he'd do the same for her.

They walked through the woods, packing the snow down under their feet.

"It's my ex," she said suddenly. She pulled off her hat, and her hair stuck straight up from static electricity. He thought she looked adorable, but she rubbed her long hair down with her hand. "He's been calling all day, which means he wants something."

"What's that?" he asked.

She shrugged. "I never know. But I'm avoiding his call because today's been so perfect."

He smiled. "It has been pretty perfect." She grinned immediately. "Well, good." She leaned her shoulder into his. "We better get a little more of the branches."

When they headed back, it was his phone that began to ring. He pulled it out from his back pocket, checking to see who was calling him. "It's Janet."

He answered it, and Janet immediately started talking.

"They're here! The trees arrived. They're out front right now."

"We'll be right there," Julian said, grasping Stephanie's hand and beginning to run. "We have to hurry."

"Where are we going?" she asked, following him down the sandy path and up to the house.

He dashed up the driveway to a flatbed truck sitting with the most gorgeous trees he had ever seen.

"They're beautiful." She squeezed his hand in hers, and Julian felt like the luckiest guy in the whole world.

"We should call for reinforcements," she said. "If you give Will the job of hanging lights, you won't be disappointed."

Julian smiled. It was a good idea. "I'll call my brother, too. He said he'd help."

She looked down at her watch. "I have to grab Asher. I could come back if my dad watches him."

"Asher is welcome here anytime, Stephanie," he said. "Anytime."

As the guys unloaded the trees, he stood there thinking about the people around him. Maybe Stephanie was right. Maybe all he needed was to lean in.

Stephanie took off while the men brought the enormous tree into the house and helped set it up. The owner of the tree farm had made a special tree stand for it.

"It sure is a beauty," Oliver said, looking up at it.

"Have you talked to Mom or Dad?" Julian asked, wondering if Oliver knew more about their visit. "I'm planning on staying at a B and B down the road while they're around," he said, wondering if they had told Oliver they were coming or if they had done the same thing to him and left him in the dark.

Oliver sighed. "Why?"

Julian didn't answer, just shrugged.

"I take it you haven't talked to them?" Oliver said.

Julian shook his head. "And, I skipped my reentrance meeting with my boss."

"You skipped the meeting Dad set up?" Oliver shook his head. "Why did you ask for it in the first place?"

"I didn't ask for it!" Julian shouted, and his voice echoed loudly throughout the room. "He wants me there. I don't want to be. He didn't even ask me. He just set it up."

"Sorry, geez." Oliver held up his hands. "I didn't know."

Julian didn't know why he'd suddenly become so incensed. But Oliver understood how Julian felt because their father had done the same thing to him when he'd quit medical school.

"I don't want to go back," Julian said.

"Then don't go back." Oliver made it sound so easy.

"I can't go back." If Julian went back, he would constantly fight his demons while working in that highly stressful career. It wasn't worth it for him. "I want to start fresh, somewhere people support me."

Oliver nodded. "You can always stay with us."

Julian shook his head. "You two just got married. The last thing you need is your brother to come and stay there on your first Christmas. Not to mention, you have a pregnant wife to think about."

"You're always welcome," Oliver said. "You know that we're all so proud of you, Jules. I think the journey you've gone on is admirable."

The knot in Julian's throat tightened so much he couldn't speak. Like he did when they were kids, Oliver patted him on the back and left his arm around Julian's shoulder. The brothers stood looking at the tree.

"The place is starting to look a lot like Christmas," Oliver said. "Thanks for doing this."

Julian nodded. "I'd do anything for you guys. I'm so happy for you."

When Stephanie and Asher returned, they brought Muriel with them. "Look who we stole from school."

Muriel and Oliver embraced as soon as they saw each other. They may still be newlyweds, but Julian felt like it was real, and he couldn't be happier for them. They were truly in love. And if he could have something, even just a little like they had, he'd be happy with that. He snuck a peek at Stephanie, who laughed with Janet about something. She looked up from tying the garland together and they locked eyes. His heart pounded inside his chest as she held his stare. There was no denying his feelings at this point.

Julian was falling for her.

By dinnertime, the house was filled with people and laughter. Stephanie, Asher, and Janet made garland while giving directions to Julian, Oliver, and Will as they hung the lights. Brandon and Cora had shown up and introduced themselves to Stephanie. Everyone helped with the decorations using the floral wire to keep the garland together, then added eucalyptus and red plaid ribbons.

As dinner approached, Janet had Billy run out to grab pizzas for everyone. They all ate and told stories of the festival. Even Oliver said he had attended the festival. "We make the shells in school with the kids."

The whole night was perfect.

Once they had wrapped the lights around all the banisters on the front porch, Oliver suggested, "We should turn the lights on."

As Asher had requested, they all marched outside in their boots to look at the lights. Julian left the front doors wide open so they could see the tree from the outside.

"It's awesome!" Asher cried out, clapping his hands in excitement. "I'm so happy!"

Julian couldn't find a better way to explain how he felt. He was happy.

But that's when he noticed Stephanie pull out her phone and silence it again, and doubt crept into the back of his mind. Because didn't Sir Isaac Newton's law of gravity say it best? What goes up must come down.

# CHAPTER 16

*A*fter spending the day decorating the Abbott house for Christmas, Stephanie fell asleep with sugar plums dancing in her head.

When she awoke, there was a bounce in her step and a text message from Julian.

**I had a great time last night.**

**I did, too.** It had been one of the most magical nights of her life. **I'm going to set up the Christmas village today.**

She had always wished her parents had added a Christmas village to their decorations. She loved looking into their tiny windows and seeing everything going on inside. All the porcelain figures looked merry and bright—perfect, just like last night.

**Will you be there?**

**No,** he answered, and her heart sank. **I have plans with a friend.**

She hoped he'd offer to meet later or the next day, but nothing more came from it. **Have fun.**

**Good luck with the village.** He sent. **My grandfather will be coming in tomorrow. He'll probably want the day to rest.**

That would be two days of not seeing Julian. She didn't want to wait that long. And what worried her was that he didn't seem eager to make plans to see her. She had thought she'd get a kiss at the end of the night, but instead, she'd gotten mixed in the shuffle of cars blocking each other and ended up leaving abruptly.

But two days?

Would the momentum from yesterday be lost? She had wanted to do more than hold his hand but hadn't wanted to push it. He didn't seem eager to rush things, and with what he had gone through over the past year, she didn't want to spook him either.

She needed to chill out.

She took a deep breath and slowly released it as she counted to eight.

She didn't think about Gabe's messages until the phone rang. She closed her eyes, knowing she couldn't avoid his calls anymore.

"Hi, Gabe," she said.

"Nice of you to answer," he said sarcastically, already picking a fight.

"Did you call for something?" she asked, but if he was calling, it was always for something.

"How've you been?" he stalled.

"Get to it, Gabe," she said.

"I'm calling for Asher," he said, stopping the formalities.

"Sure," she said but didn't move from her room. This was their strained relationship. Two bickering adults who held resentments of each other. She had every right to hate him. He was a cheater and a liar. The best con man she had ever come across. But he was also Asher's dad. They'd be connected whether they liked each other or not. She had to let go of her anger, for Asher. "Let me go get him."

She knocked on Asher's bedroom door.

"Come in!"

She opened the door, holding out the phone. "It's your dad."

Asher jumped up from his toys on the floor and took the phone. He immediately put it on speaker, a habit he'd started when he was little. She wasn't sure if Gabe realized this fact or not, but he didn't seem to care one way or another.

"Hey, kiddo," he said in his fake voice. "How's it going?"

"Good," Asher said, still unable to keep a conversation on the telephone.

"How's school?" Gabe asked.

"Good."

Stephanie wondered what he wanted.

"So, kiddo, I was thinking you could come to my house for Christmas this year," Gabe said. "What do you think of that?"

"What?" she said out loud.

"Stephanie?" Gabe said.

"Give me the phone, Asher." She held out her hand.

"It's not up to Mom, kiddo. It's up to you," Gabe said as she shut the phone off. How dare he ask Asher to Christmas?

"Why'd you hang up on Dad?" Asher asked.

She didn't know how to be honest without breaking his heart. Gabe's number lit up her screen as he tried calling again. "Just because . . . it's an adult conversation."

Her answer didn't seem to satisfy him. "I wish you guys could get along like you and Jules do."

And her heart tore.

"Let me talk to dad, okay?" She left Asher's room and dialed Gabe's number. "I can't believe you asked him without talking to me first."

"I'm his father, and I haven't spent one Christmas with him since I got back," he said, but that wasn't true. When he'd returned from his last tour, he could have spent time with Asher and her on Christmas, but he had chosen to go out and drink.

"You need to call my lawyer before you go making plans." What would Asher want to do? Would he want to go with Gabe? The fun guy who buys him things and lets him eat whatever he wants. He's the one who takes him everywhere to meet all his friends and lets him stay up late. Gabe's the one who doesn't make him do all the other stuff like clean up and brush his teeth.

How much more pain could she endure from this man?

"You asked him to come to Christmas without even thinking about the ramifications."

"Are you thinking about Asher or are you thinking about yourself?" he said.

She saw red. "Call my lawyer from now on."

She ran down the hall to the bathroom before someone saw her break down. She didn't want Asher to see her cry, but her heart tore apart at the thought of not spending Christmas with him.

Would a Navy veteran who'd gone on two tours and still volunteered for the local fire department get custody over a woman who was in between jobs? Would it matter if he never came around like he promised? She knew that after Christmas, he'd get bored with being a father and drop Asher off when he became an inconvenience. She'd have to pick up the pieces, and Asher would revert to being afraid of her leaving too.

"Steph?" her dad called from outside the door. "You, okay?"

"Yes," she said with as happy of a voice she could muster, then covered her face with a towel to muffle her cries. "I'm fine."

"Okay. Because it sounds like you're crying," her father said.

She swung the door open. "Do you think I'm a loser?"

"What?" He clearly didn't understand that his daughter was falling apart. "No, I don't think you're a loser."

"But when I got pregnant, did you think I was a loser?" She didn't know why she was asking this.

"No."

She stared at him, wishing more than anything that her mom was here to talk to. She loved her father, but it was her mother who had understood her. She wrapped her arms around his neck and cried.

"Gabe wants to take Asher for Christmas."

"He's not going to get Asher for Christmas,' he said patting her on the back and releasing her. "Come on, Stephanie, put on your game face. Asher will get scared if he sees you upset."

"I don't want him to go." She sniffled. "And what if he tries to get more than just Christmas? You know how much everyone loves Gabe. Half the town still blames me for him sleeping with all those women during our marriage."

"Stop," her father said. "He's not getting Asher. Now go get cleaned up, and I'll get Asher ready for school."

She took a long shower, crying the whole time, imagining waking up to an empty house with nothing under the tree.

And was it fair that she got Asher? The reality was, Gabe was his father. He probably felt the same sadness.

But Asher was her something special.

When she got out of the bathroom, Asher waited for her to talk.

"Am I going to Dad's for Christmas?" he asked, and she could see his anxiety turning the wheels in his head with question after question.

"How do you feel about going there for Christmas?" In the end, all she wanted was what was best for Asher.

"Won't Santa get confused?"

She shook her head. "We'll tell him."

"But that means I won't have Christmas here?" he asked.

She nodded, trying to hold her tears in. She hoped he'd stop with the questions, because she couldn't talk.

"I don't want to go to Dad's. What if we all went to Jules's like last night?" Asher said it like he had found the perfect solution, which only made her heart tear further.

How had she gotten so lucky with such a sweet, special boy?

"I think Julian will have his own family at the house." She thought about inviting Julian to her Christmas. Then she thought about meeting his parents. How would they feel if they found out he'd been hanging out with the staff? From what she'd heard, his parents would probably have a problem with it. But she was more than staff to him, right?

She was glad she wouldn't see Julian at the house that day, because she hadn't stopped crying all morning. Her eyes were swollen and red and bloodshot. She looked and felt horrible and couldn't stop worrying about what might happen.

"What is going on?" Lindy asked as soon as she walked into the diner.

She sniffled through a hiccup. "Gabe wants Asher to stay with him for Christmas."

"Oh, honey," Lindy said. "When was the last time that deadbeat even saw Asher?"

Her breath shook as she answered, "Last Easter."

"And now he wants Asher for Christmas?" Lindy came straight over to Stephanie and hugged her. "If I see that sorry son of a b—"

"Lindy, it's fine. Asher is his son too." Stephanie had scripted what to say in situations like this. Everyone in town knew her story. The second she said or did anything that involved Gabe, it became big gossip. She never knew whether people were on Team Stephanie or Team Gabe. Both were born and raised in Blueberry Bay, and half the town was related to them somehow.

Her bottom lip quivered when she said, "I'll be okay."

Lindy shook her head. "Do you need to take the day off?"

Stephanie shook her head. She couldn't afford to do that with Christmas coming. But even with two jobs, she couldn't give Asher the Christmas he deserved. All she wanted was for him to be happy. So, if that meant sucking up her feelings and letting him spend Christmas with Gabe, then she'd have to do it.

"I'll be fine." She patted a wet paper towel on her face and got back to work.

But the whole day, she'd thought about the phone call with Gabe and how determined he sounded. He never fought for Asher, so why now? She called her lawyer during lunch and went to Lindy to ask for some extra hours.

"I thought you were quitting?" Lindy said, half joking. She took a pencil and scribbled Stephanie's name into the calendar. "Can you take Saturday, second shift?"

The festival was on Saturday. She'd miss the beginning, but still make it in time for Santa. "Sure, I can take it."

"What's your schedule going to be working for the Abbotts?" Lindy asked.

Stephanie had asked Janet about her work schedule, but all Janet had said was that she made her hours work around the Abbotts's schedule, which gave Stephanie no answer. All she knew was that she only had to work at night if requested; otherwise, she could leave to pick Asher up.

"What's the cute Abbott like?" Brenda, another server, asked. "I heard he's like, a drunk."

"That's not true," Stephanie snapped at her. She had heard people call Julian worse things before. She had probably repeated those things. She had even told stories about when he'd come over as a kid. But now, she wouldn't allow it.

"Well, isn't someone getting their panties in a bunch," Brenda said as a joke, but it only upset Stephanie further.

Stephanie normally would've let it go and apologized for speaking up, but this time, she was ready to fight.

"He's not a drunk, and it's a really mean thing to say about someone you don't know," Stephanie scolded. Brenda may be older, but Stephanie was a woman who would speak up for the people she loved.

And that was the moment she realized how far she had fallen.

"Somebody has a little crush." Brenda cackled, which made her feel a little embarrassed because a customer, Bryce Zhang, was sitting nearby, overhearing the conversation.

*Just let it go*, Stephanie said in her head. *Just let it go.*

"He practically bought out my toy store," Bryce said from the counter. "Walked in to buy a gift and ended up buying half my inventory for the festival."

Brenda's scowl twisted deeper on her face.

"Do you remember when they threw those grand Christmas balls at the house?" Stephanie asked Bryce, the long-time owner of one of the oldest shops in Blueberry Bay. He had to have been around then.

"Oh goodness, I haven't thought about those in years," Bryce said. "It was Mrs. Abbott, if I recall, who threw them. I don't even remember seeing Max there. But they were spectacular. She even had a fireworks show at the end of the evening."

"And the whole town was invited?" she asked.

"Yes, everybody." Bryce pointed at Lindy. "You went to a few."

Lindy nodded. "Gorgeous events. We'd all look forward to it."

"What happened? Why did they stop?" Stephanie figured they'd stopped over twenty-five years ago.

Lindy shrugged. "I don't know, but they just stopped one year."

Stephanie left her shift at Lindy's and headed straight for the Abbotts'. She had a few hours before she needed to get home.

She parked in her regular spot and noticed a fancy black car. A man in a black suit sat in the driver's seat, as if waiting for someone.

She didn't know who it was, but she immediately started to worry. What if his parents had decided to come early?

When she walked in, she heard a deep voice and laughter coming from Janet's office. She knew who it was before Max Abbott came out.

"You must be the lovely Stephanie," he said, reaching out his hand. "You look just like you did as a child."

The white-haired man stood tall. Even in his late seventies, he was attractive and clearly took care of himself. His large hand enveloped hers as he shook it.

"I've heard nothing but glowing reviews of your work," he said, looking back at Janet.

Stephanie smiled at Janet. She wasn't sure if Janet liked her most days, but she appreciated the positive feedback.

"It's been great working here," she said.

He looked around the kitchen and pointed to the centerpiece

on the table. "It looks just like it did when Corrine would decorate," he said.

His chin started to wobble, and Stephanie was sure if this man started crying, she would as well.

"It's just like Corrine," he said again, walking through to the dining room and stopping in front of the boxes for the village she had left.

"I was just about to put out the Christmas village," she said, getting in front of Mr. Abbott and picking up some of the boxes to make a path to walk. "Sorry about the mess."

"No need to apologize." He kept going through to the front hall.

Stephanie looked at Janet as she followed him. She quietly said, "I thought he was coming tomorrow."

Janet mouthed back, "Me too." Then, she held her palms up as if she had no explanation.

Stephanie put the boxes down and followed them.

"I'm looking forward to seeing it all lit up tonight." He turned to Janet. "Where's Julian?"

"He's in the city," Janet answered.

"What?" Stephanie said too quickly, and they both looked at her. "I thought he was here."

Janet shook her head. "He left for Boston this morning."

"When's he coming back?" Mr. Abbott asked.

She wanted to know the same thing. Had he decided to leave after all? But wouldn't he have said something to her? And why had he told her he was hanging out with a friend if he was going to Boston?

"He thought he was picking you up at the airport," she said. "Didn't you call him and tell him you were coming?"

Mr. Abbott shook his head. "I wanted to beat the storm coming in. Besides, I just couldn't take the heat. I wanted to see some snow." He walked to the lounge and opened the door. "You might as well tell our new girl here what happens when I'm in here."

148

"Don't bother him," Janet told Stephanie as the doors closed.

"Even if there's an emergency?" Stephanie didn't like that idea.

"Well, use your discretion," Janet said. "The only time I interrupted his lounge time was when there was a fire, so that should tell you something."

"There was a fire?" Stephanie hadn't thought about what to do if the house caught on fire.

"Just a small kitchen fire," Janet said, returning to the kitchen. "When Mr. Abbott's home, I try to give him as much space and privacy as possible. This is his refuge." She quietly said, "I know Julian said you could bring Asher these last few times, and since you've given up your nights, I didn't say anything, but I would not expect you to be able to bring Asher whenever you want."

Stephanie suddenly became embarrassed. She wouldn't have brought Asher if all those circumstances weren't true. She hadn't planned on bringing her child to work, but they had asked her to give up her evenings to train. What was she supposed to do if she didn't have a babysitter?

"Are you okay?" Janet asked, snapping Stephanie out of her spiraling thoughts.

*Let it go*, she thought. *Let it go.*

"Yes, I'm fine," she said.

"Are you sure you're alright?"

Stephanie nodded, faking it. "I'm fine."

But she wasn't fine. Now, her thoughts were spinning about Julian.

"When you're done with the village, let me know," Janet said, "and I'll show you what January and February will look like."

Stephanie removed the individual houses from each box. Mrs. Abbott had displayed her village on the shelves in the china hutch. She looked at the long stretch of wall where the hutch had been built. Dozens of expensive dishes, platters, bowls, and cups were on display. What would she do with all of the dishes?

She looked back at the boxes sitting on the floor. There had to be over fifty of them, plus the snow and outside items like trees and figures of people and families happily walking around. She had to set up an ice-skating rink, and the church took three pieces, and a glass shelf needed to be removed to fit it all in.

She stood staring at everything, not knowing where to start.

"You just have to go for it," Oliver said.

She jumped as soon as she heard his voice. "Oh my goodness, you scared me."

"Sorry." He held up his hand. "I came in from the back."

"Can I get you anything?" she asked, not knowing what to do in this situation.

Oliver shook his head. "I'm here to see my grandfather."

"He's in the lounge." She nodded to the closed doors.

"I know, that's why I'm bothering you," he said with a smile. He knew the rule too. "What did he think of the decorations?"

She opened up a box and pulled out a bakery. "He looked happy."

Oliver seemed pleased by this. "Good. That's good."

"Yeah," she said.

"He didn't want it out for years," Oliver said.

"He didn't want it out?" Now she thought back to Janet's panic.

"I wanted it out to show Muriel." He walked to where she stood. "Can you keep a secret?"

She smiled. "Of course."

"We're having a baby," he whispered, holding his finger to his lips. "So, I wanted to show her what an Abbott Christmas used to look like. And we're going to announce the baby when everyone's together."

She hoped Julian would come back for that. "That's wonderful news. Congratulations."

"I'm really excited," Oliver said. "And what better time of the year to celebrate than Christmas?"

"Absolutely," she said.

"I'm going to enter the lounge," he said, gesturing toward the door. "Wish me luck."

"Good luck," she said back.

He chuckled and left the room. It took her two hours to remove the dishes and then another hour to arrange the plugs and all the extension cords. By almost seven o'clock, she decided to call it quits. She stepped down from the ladder when she heard someone coming.

Max Abbott stood at the dining room entrance, looking at her work.

"I need to go home," she said, "and put my son to bed. I can come back and finish it when he's asleep."

"Janet says you waited tables at the diner," Mr. Abbott said.

"Yes." She hoped he'd consider that work experience.

"I was sorry you didn't finish college," he said. "You were always such a bright young lady."

She hadn't expected him to remember her or be interested enough in her education, but didn't he know her story like everyone else in town?

"I had a baby and couldn't afford school." She looked at the boxes, hoping he'd tell her if he wanted her to return.

"Julian said you have a great son."

"He's a good boy," she responded, unsure how much Julian had told his grandfather. Would he give her the same speech Janet had about bringing Asher to the house? She hoped not.

"He's a sweet boy. Just has to figure out his path," he said, initially confusing her, until she realized he was talking about Julian.

She nodded, not sure how to respond.

"He's always had a lot of distractions in his life," he continued.

Was he going to say something about her and Julian? Would she lose her job? What was she thinking holding hands with a guy like him? He was way too good for her. Look at the house! Their houses for the Christmas village were nicer than her family's home.

She looked at her watch, hoping he'd end the conversation.

With school tomorrow, she didn't want Asher to stay up later than he should be.

"He's been a bit lost lately," he carried on. "But taking a position at his father's company is what he needs to do, not hide at his grandfather's summer house."

She wanted to tell him that Julian didn't want to work at the firm. That he wanted to stay in Maine not to hide, but to live. She didn't though. She said nothing.

"Didn't you say you needed to go?" he asked her.

She nodded. "Would you like me to come back?"

She prayed he'd say no.

"If you don't mind finishing it up," he said, walking toward the kitchen now. "I'm going to grab myself some of Janet's special hot chocolate. You'll have to ask her how to make it before she leaves."

As Stephanie raced home the last thing she wanted to do after working a full shift at the diner and five hours at the Abbotts' was go back and work well past midnight. What was she thinking offering to come back? Why didn't she just say she was coming back tomorrow. Because the Abbott name intimidated her. She wondered if taking this job was a big mistake.

Or if holding hands with Julian was the mistake.

# CHAPTER 17

*A* fire glowed in the sitting room as Father Michael ushered Julian inside the church's rectory. "You made it just before the storm."

"Yeah, I didn't realize there was a nor'easter coming in." Julian wished he had planned better.

"How've you been?" Father Michael said once they sat down. He began pouring coffee for both of them, the same way Brandon did when they were together. The men had a bond so strong that Julian hardly had to say anything for Father Michael to understand.

"I met someone," he said.

"Ah." Father Michael didn't need to hear more. The rehabilitation program didn't encourage relationships for at least the first year of sobriety. He needed to work on himself before he could commit to someone else.

"I've fallen for her hard." Julian had no trouble speaking the truth to the priest. Something about his calm demeanor and his forgiving nature made it easy. A recovering alcoholic himself, Father Michael understood things nondrinkers didn't. But this confession felt different. He wanted Father Michael to tell him what to do, but deep down, he knew he wouldn't.

"I thought there was a reason why you wanted to see me." Father Michael placed the coffee pot down and passed a saucer and delicately placed cup to Julian. "What's her name?"

"Stephanie," he said.

Father Michael nodded. "It's been over a year. Do you feel ready for a relationship?"

Julian didn't. "That's why I'm here."

"I can't tell you when you're ready." Father Michael laughed. "You're the only one who will know. But first, tell me why you're acting all weird."

"I am?" Julian dropped his head into his hands. "My grandfather showed up at the house this afternoon and met her. I wanted to be there when he came, but he showed up early."

"Why did you want to be there when they met?" Father Michael asked.

"Because she's working for our family." Julian heard it now— the unprofessionalism of the whole thing. The warning Janet had given him. His father would lose his mind when he heard about it. He just wanted to tell his grandfather before everything blew up in his face, because everything always did.

"My father will not see it as a relationship. He'll see it as a money grab or a lawsuit waiting to happen." Julian wished he could've been there when she'd met his grandfather. "I wanted to be there to set the tone. To make it clear that she's not just our house manager but someone I've become very close with."

Julian was sure his father wouldn't care about his son's feelings. The last time Julian had talked to his father about a woman was when he'd told him about Cora.

Father Michael shifted his position in his seat, and the chair creaked underneath him. "Maybe your father will surprise you."

"Does a leopard change its spots?" Julian said right back. "It won't matter that she's kind and a good mother—that'll just be another strike against her. It won't matter that she's a hard worker or cares about the people around her, or that she makes you feel comfortable around her. He'll see what he wants to see."

"Maybe talk to him?" Father Michael always went the communication route. "You might be making this whole worst-case scenario up in your head."

"My father never changes," Julian said. "Ever."

He had worn the same clothing style since entering the business world thirty years ago. He had the same haircut, the same drinks at night, and the same secretary since he'd started. The man didn't believe he needed to change, because he thought he was perfect already.

"You might be surprised," Father Michael said.

"Doubt it." Julian took a sip of coffee. "He wants me to go back to the company. He wants me to be someone I'm not anymore or really ever was."

"Well, that's not up to him." Father Michael leaned forward in his chair to get closer to Julian. "Who do you want to be? That's what I'd be worried about right now. Who do you want to be?"

"That's the thing," he said. "I don't know who I am."

"Did I ever tell you when I decided to become a priest?" Father Michael said.

"No, when did you know?" Julian asked.

Father Michael started to laugh. "When my dad came home from the bars, he'd be a real mean son of a gun, if you know what I mean. He'd come into the house stinking the place up, yelling at my mom for something totally ridiculous, and one night my mother invited the local priest to our house for supper. He came in, my father showed up raging drunk, and he began the whole thing, coming in loud, stinking, and yelling at my mom. But then he saw the priest sitting in his seat, and my dad totally changed his tune. The priest told him how disappointed he was. How he needed to take care of his wife and children. How important it was for him to be a good father and husband. My father acted completely different around him. Even helped clean up after dinner. When the priest left, I told my mother I wanted to be that guy."

Julian smiled, thinking of a little Father Michael.

"But when I became a priest, I had started drinking more and more. The pressure to meet everyone's expectations made me drink more. When I hit my lowest, I realized I wasn't the super-hero in my story who had come in to save the day. I was the guy who came in and stunk up the place. I knew I needed a different path."

That hit Julian.

"That's the thing about recovery," Father Michael said. "You have to find your new path. It's a little less broken in and feels unfamiliar and uncomfortable. But it's yours and yours alone."

Julian didn't know what path he was on, but he hoped he was at least on the right one.

Before leaving the city, he had to stop by his old apartment to pick up a few things. He wanted to grab some of his winter stuff, especially his boots, to be a good example for Asher. He could take more of his other things.

The condo had an industrial look, long, sleek lines, stainless steel appliances and hardware, black marble floors, and black leather furniture. It was a bachelor's paradise but not a home. It felt cold and dark. He didn't even want to stay there.

He grabbed a suitcase and started throwing clothes inside. He looked out the window, and the snow that had started that after-noon now fell down faster and looked heavier. He didn't want to stay, but he'd have to wait it out. Blueberry Bay was at least five or more hours up 95. He'd be stupid to drive it, especially in his sedan, even if it was all-wheel drive.

He turned on the news. "Storm warnings are out across the city. At least eight to twelve inches are expected to come in overnight and into tomorrow morning's commute. Roads are already slick with the heavy snow. If you have to go out, drive safe. It's a mess out there."

He turned off the television. He wouldn't be able to leave until tomorrow at the earliest.

He hoped he'd get back in time for the festival. He didn't want to miss that.

A text came through on his phone.

**Finally, I finished**, Stephanie wrote, with a picture of the Christmas village attached. It looked incredible—precisely the way his grandmother had set it up every year.

**I wish I had been there when my grandfather saw the place.** He was disappointed, to say the least.

**He got emotional in a good way.** She sent it with a pink heart emoji.

**Thank you for everything.** He wished he could say it in person.

**Don't tell me you're going to miss the Christmas festival?**

**I'm stuck in Boston because of the storm, but I will leave when the roads are clear.**

**Good.**

And his heart did that thing it did every time he saw her smile or look at him.

**I can't wait to see you.**

**Me too.**

As he stood in the middle of his condo, things suddenly became crystal clear. He no longer belonged in Boston. Or in this condo. Or at Diversified Business and Credit.

His future felt strange and unfamiliar. He was uncomfortable not knowing what came next, but he'd have to figure things out because he knew he couldn't stay here anymore.

He looked out at the night. He opened the doors to the balcony, which had one of the best views of Boston. When he'd bought the place, he'd thought he needed it to show off his success. The view, the car, the title, the girl—but none of it mattered to him anymore.

He looked up at the sky as the snow fell silently around him. The whole world seemed to be still. No traffic or honking. No shouting or sirens blaring. And in that quiet, Julian imagined a new life with Stephanie and Asher and found his new path.

He spent the rest of the night looking up lobster boats. Used lobster boats, new custom-built boats, and anything on the web located close enough to look at. Then he texted Will before he could regret anything.

**What if I took you up on that sponsorship?**

# CHAPTER 18

*I*t turned out that going back and working on the Christmas village had been the best decision Stephanie could've made. Max Abbott was quite the talker once he left the lounge.

"You kids were always up to something," he told her as he sat at the dining room table. He laughed. "I remember when Julian and your brother built a raft and took off in the ocean."

"I forgot about their Huckleberry Finn stage." She laughed at the memory. "Would you like another cup of cocoa?" she asked, but he shook his head.

"I'll be up all night using the bathroom," he said. "How long have you been at it?"

"The village?" she asked, and he nodded. "A while."

He let out a laugh. "I think Corrine added more and more each year so she didn't have to deal with me all the time. I always used to feel cooped up during the winter."

"She really loved Christmas." That couldn't be denied after reading through the binders. "Have you seen everything with the lights on?" she asked him.

He shook his head. "I haven't gone outside. I can't remember where I put my jacket and boots."

She snuck a peek at her watch. It was after ten o'clock. She didn't need to rush, not with the snow coming down like it was. "Why don't I find them? We can go out there together."

Finding a coat that would work with gloves and a hat didn't take long. She helped put his arms in the sleeves and feet in the boots. He took her arm as they went outside and the reflection from the lights on the snow guided their way. She had thought she had seen the house enough times, but when she turned around, it still took her breath away. A layer of snow covered some of the lights, making the snow glow from underneath. Each bush and tree had lights wrapped around them. The only sound was the waves clapping against the shore.

Mr. Abbott's chin quivered as he looked at the house. "You've done a marvelous job, Corrine."

She smiled at him, not correcting him. She'd let him have this moment. She held on to his arm as tears ran down his face. Her breath iridescent under the lights.

"Just a beautiful job." His eyes danced around, looking at the house. He reminded her of a little kid staring at the Christmas tree—the joy of Christmas showed in his delighted face.

"Why don't I take you to bed," she said. "You must be exhausted from all that traveling."

"Don't tell me you're putting up more decorations," Mr. Abbott told her. He looked at her differently, casually, as though he knew her.

"Not tonight," she said to him.

"My Corrine, the Christmas elf," he said, holding her arm.

Slowly, she walked Max Abbott back into the house and up the stairs to his master. By the time he reached the door, he seemed lucid again, recognizing her as the maid, not his deceased wife.

"I'm very tired," he said.

"Are you feeling alright?" she asked, wishing Julian was here. "Julian is stuck in the city tonight. Will you be okay?"

"Oh, sure," he said, opening the door to his room, but he didn't move, holding onto her. "I've forgotten where the light switch is."

She reached into the dark room and hit the switch, trying hard not to make judgments. He had just come home from Florida, she reminded herself. Anyone would be disoriented after a long day. Besides, hadn't he spent the last few months away? He probably legitimately forgot where the light switch had been.

But when he asked her to help turn down the bed, she wondered how much he had changed since the last time he had seen Julian.

She hadn't expected to stay the night, but when her father called, she knew he was right.

"You shouldn't be driving in this," he said.

She looked out at the snow. "What about Asher? He'll be freaked out if I'm not there."

"He'll be just fine because Will and I are here," her dad said. "Besides, there are plenty of rooms to sleep in that place."

"I think it's probably best," she said. "Mr. Abbott is a little disorientated."

"Where's Julian?" her dad asked.

"He's in the city," she said.

"Doing what?"

"I'm not exactly sure." She hadn't asked him. He'd tell her if he wanted her to know. All that mattered was that he was coming back. "But he's stuck because of the snow. Can you make sure Asher's okay without me tonight?"

Her dad snorted. "Watching his grandfather is an awfully big ask."

"I don't feel right leaving him all alone," she said. "What if the power goes out? He might need help."

That was a very real possibility.

"I've got Asher, don't worry," her dad said. "Just be safe."

"I will." She looked around the kitchen. She should wake Mr.

Abbott up and tell him she was still there. She should ask if she should stay.

"What are you doing, Corrine?" Mr. Abbott's voice came from the other side of the room. "I thought you were coming to bed."

Stephanie jumped and turned to face him.

"Oh, you're not Corrine," he said, shaking his head. "Excuse me."

"I haven't left because of the snow," she explained, feeling silly asking him to stay.

"You should stay in the guest room," he offered without thinking twice. "Corrine will make it up."

She smiled. "Can I get you something?"

"My mother always made me warm milk when I couldn't sleep," he said.

"Would you like me to heat some up for you?" she asked, walking over to him.

He started to shuffle toward the front hall. "I think I'll sit in the lounge and look at the Christmas tree."

The six-foot tree had been placed in the lounge next to the fireplace. It was decorated with handmade ornaments all the children and grandchildren had made over the years. Pictures of the family, handprints made in clay, drawings, and popsicle sticks hung on the tree. It was missing only one thing—a shell ornament.

She walked with him to the lounge.

"Looks like we need a fire," he said, pointing to the dark fireplace.

"I can start that for you," she said, helping him sit in his recliner.

"That would be marvelous," he said, groaning as he sat.

"So, you can't sleep?" she asked as she placed the logs in the fireplace.

"I'm afraid the seasons are changing," he answered but didn't elaborate.

Stephanie wasn't exactly sure what he meant but left it at that.

She crumpled up some newspaper and stuffed it under the logs like her father would do. It didn't take long for the fire to come to life. When she was sure it would continue to burn, she turned to Mr. Abbott, holding his armrest, and said, "Let me get that glass of milk."

He placed his hand on hers. "I've missed you, Corrine."

She smiled, letting him hold her hand as her heart sank. She didn't want to break this man's heart, but would pretending to be his dead wife make things worse? She picked up a throw blanket from the couch. "Would you like a blanket?"

He looked up from the fireplace. "You've done a beautiful job with the house."

The rule of not disturbing Max Abbott while in the lounge went out the chimney that night. Stephanie made his warm milk and sat in the recliner next to him, where she imagined Corrine used to sit, and made sure he was okay. He slept like a baby in his recliner, hardly stirring at all.

When early morning arrived, she made sure to wake him carefully.

"Mr. Abbott, it's Stephanie, the house manager," she said, gently rubbing his hand to wake him. "Let me help you up to your bedroom."

"Did I fall asleep here last night?" he asked, unaware she had stayed with him the whole time.

He carefully got up with her assistance and looked out the window. "It's beautiful."

"We got at least twelve inches, maybe more," she said. "We're lucky we didn't lose power."

He nodded, his hand tremoring in her hold. "I think I should go back to bed."

She helped Mr. Abbott back to his room. When she returned downstairs, she picked up the lounge and made sure the fire was out. She picked up her phone. She should call Julian. Tell him about last night and his grandfather. She wasn't a doctor, but he didn't seem well, traveling or not. He wasn't someone who should be living alone in this big old house.

And as she heard the scraping of the plow coming up the drive, she could feel her new job being scraped away with it.

# CHAPTER 19

*J*ulian raced up 95 as soon as the roads were clear. His stomach twisted with nerves and excitement. He went to text Stephanie that he was on his way, when he saw she had texted him about staying at the house because of the weather. He wondered if his grandfather had been accommodating or had sat in his lounge completely ignoring her. Either way, he hoped things hadn't changed for Stephanie, because, if anything, he was more in than ever.

The regular drive was long enough, but add in a nor'easter and snow cleanup, and the five-hour drive had taken more than eight by the time he pulled off the exit for Blueberry Bay. Another text pinged his phone. It was Will this time.

**We need to talk.**

Julian didn't like the sound of that. No greeting or salutation. Not even an emoji to give reference to his feelings one way or another.

Julian pulled over as soon as he saw the local gas station and called Will.

When Julian had texted Will the night before, he hadn't responded. He wondered if Will never expected Julian to accept his offer and now regretted it. Maybe he didn't want to get stuck with him on the water all day. Perhaps he thought Julian would be soft out on the boat. Maybe he thought Julian was crazy.

"I think it's best if we talk later," Will said as soon as he answered. "I'm headed to the festival with Asher."

He noticed that Will, who always invited him to everything, hadn't. "Mind if I join you?"

"Were you in the right state of mind last night when you asked me about sponsoring you?" Will asked.

"No, man. I'm serious," Julian said. "I want this."

"You went out a couple of days." Will snorted into the phone. "It's a two-year commitment."

"I've always wanted to do this," Julian said, thinking about all those days in his office or at school wishing he could be a LaBelle. Have a family that loved and supported you.

"Hold on, man." Will's voice sounded muffled. "I need some privacy, Ash, okay?"

Julian heard the squeak of a door closing shut.

"Are you there?" Will asked.

"Yeah, I'm here." Julian's mouth went dry waiting for Will to finish his thought.

"It's just that I can't have you break Stephanie's heart," Will said. "I can't watch her and Asher think you're going to stick around, because we know that's not true, don't we? I mean, you couldn't even stick around to finish helping her with your grandfather."

"I was stuck because of the snow," Julian protested. "I wanted to come back."

"Look, she's been through enough with Gabe," Will said. He wasn't listening to Julian's excuses. "I won't have another man come in and mess with her."

"I had to see my sponsor, to talk about her," Julian confessed. He banged his head against the steering wheel. He didn't like this feeling. The feeling of vulnerability. "I wanted to make sure I'm a good enough man for her."

"Are you thinking of drinking again?" Will said, but he didn't wait for Julian to answer. "Because if you start drinking again—"

"I want to be with Stephanie," he interrupted Will. He caught his breath at the anxiety from his confession. "And I wanted to make sure I'm ready for a commitment. That's why I went to the city."

Will didn't say anything for what felt like forever.

"Dude, come on," Julian said.

"How serious can Julian Abbott be about a local girl?" Will said, full of doubt.

"I'm in love with her." He waited, closing his eyes as if Will's fist could go through the phone.

But only silence could be heard on the other end. "She's at the diner tonight. She picked up some extra shifts. She'll be the one who you'll need to talk to about getting sponsored."

Will hung up after that, and Julian didn't know what that meant. Had something happened between when he'd left and now? He didn't have time to figure it out; he needed to see Stephanie. He pulled out of the gas station and headed toward the diner.

When he pulled into the diner, he walked right in and looked for Stephanie. As he peered around the room, a woman with a gray bun on her head approached him. "Good evening. Are you meeting somebody?"

"I'm looking for Stephanie LaBelle." He didn't see her.

"You just missed her," the woman said. "She said she was headed to your house."

He forgot how everyone knew everyone in this town. "She did?"

She nodded. "She said something about taking your grandfather to the festival."

He laughed in relief. "Really?"

She nodded again.

"Okay, wow. Alright then. Thanks." He left the diner feeling completely overwhelmed by the last twenty-four hours. He picked up his phone and called her.

"Hey," she said, answering right away.

"Hey," he said back, a wave of calm washing over him at the sound of her voice.

"Are you still in Boston?"

"I'm sitting outside the diner," he said, looking inside.

"You are? I just left."

"I know." He smiled, hearing her happy tone. "You're picking up my grandfather to take him to the festival."

"I am," she said. "Is that okay?"

"Of course it's okay!" He laughed at that. "He's lucky you like him enough to take him."

"He said he hasn't gone since he was a little kid." She said this as if it were a travesty. "I had to offer when he told me that."

"What about your family?" he asked.

"We're all going together," she said. "Oliver said Muriel wasn't feeling well tonight, so I offered to take your grandfather since the diner was dead."

"That's really nice of you." He honestly couldn't think of anything kinder.

"Should we meet you there?" she asked.

He smiled. "Yes. Meet me at the Ferris wheel."

# CHAPTER 20

*A*fter hearing all the gossip and opinions of the Abbotts, Max turned out to be nothing like she'd expected. He was very caring. All he wanted to do was love and support his family. Sure, he had thought she was his late wife last night, but he had been nothing but welcoming when he'd met her.

When he went back to bed that morning, she was worried. As soon as she left his room, she called Janet.

"Can you stay with him until Julian can get there?" Janet asked.

"I need to get home to Asher," she said.

"I'd come and relieve you; it's just that we've got broken power lines across our driveway, and I'm afraid I can't get out," Janet explained.

Stephanie tapped her nails against the counter. "I'll figure things out."

"Thanks, Stephanie," Janet said. "You are a lifesaver."

She called Will right after she talked to Janet.

"I'm afraid I can't watch Asher," Will said. "Dad and I have to check on our boats, and we can't have him around. It's not safe."

He was right. "Just bring Asher here."

She'd deal with the consequences if Mr. Abbott wasn't cool

about her bringing Asher, because there was no way she could leave Max in the state he was in.

"Mr. Abbott?" She knocked on his door. "Do you need anything?"

She heard him take a breath, but he stayed quiet.

"It's me, Stephanie, the new house manager," she said as gently as possible. She wasn't sure if he remembered her or not. "Can I get you anything for breakfast?"

"Yes, please. That would be kind of you."

"I'm going to have to bring my son here if you'd like my help today. My brother and father can't watch him because of the storm."

"Where's Janet?" he said.

"She's stuck at home," she said, "power lines across her driveway." She wondered if he worried that he was stuck with her like she was worried she was stuck with him.

"How about my grandson? Is he home?"

"No, I'm afraid he's still in the city." Silence again. She felt terrible. "I can make breakfast for you. Would you like me to invite Oliver and Muriel over?"

"No, no, they should stay put with the snow," he said, his voice a bit peppier. "Make enough breakfast for you and your son."

She smiled when he said that. She didn't know much about Mr. Abbott. It now seemed strange that Janet didn't have a binder on just him—what he liked, what he ate besides his breakfast setup, and all his other preferences.

She rummaged through the pantry, looking for a list of used meals or recipes. She checked the different foods and goods on the shelves, trying to figure out what he would like for breakfast.

She couldn't find anything, so she decided to use her go-to— her mom's recipes.

She grabbed the eggs and the fresh English muffins. She pulled out the mixer and began separating the eggs for the hollandaise sauce. From the refrigerator, she grabbed some bacon they had bought at a local farm that would be a perfect substitute for the Canadian sliced bacon she typically used for her mother's famous eggs Benedict.

After twenty minutes, breakfast was almost ready, and Will pulled up to the house with Asher in the backseat of his truck. She rushed to the door and kissed Asher all over as soon as he got out of the truck, then led him to the mudroom to remove all his winter things.

"Did you bring slippers?" she asked.

Will looked at her like she was crazy. "You're lucky he brushed his teeth."

She kissed Will on the cheek. "Thank you so much for taking care of him last night."

"Geez, Mom, it was only a night," Asher said, going into the kitchen with his backpack.

She turned to Will. "How was it last night?"

"It was fine," he said.

The word fine set off red flags. "What's wrong?"

"Nothing," he said, looking in the other direction. He walked toward the office and peeked inside. When he came back around, he said, "Dad said Julian took off for the city."

"Yeah, he had some things he needed to do," she said.

"But he didn't tell you he left?" Will asked.

She could feel her defenses rise. "Yeah, so?"

"So that's Julian's typical MO," Will said, crossing his arms.

"Don't you have to check on your boat?" she asked.

"Look, I saw you two the other night looking at each other," Will whispered, his back to Asher. "Just watch out because he'll love you and then take off. It's what he does."

She couldn't believe her brother. Just when she thought he had changed, he was bossing her around, thinking the worst of everyone.

"First of all, he has no obligation to stay in Blueberry Bay," she said. "Secondly, it's none of our business what he does with his personal life.

"Come on, Stephanie, I'm not blind," he said louder than she wanted him to.

Asher looked up from his toys on the table.

"Don't empty that bag," she said to Asher. "We're having breakfast here, and Mommy needs your help cooking today."

"He didn't even stay home for his grandfather," Will said, throwing his hand out.

"He didn't even know his grandfather was coming," she argued. But nothing seemed to matter with Will at the moment. She put her hand on his shoulder. She knew what this was about. He was afraid of losing his best friend again. "Maybe have a little faith in him."

"What if he were to stay?" Will asked. "Do you like him?"

"Are we in middle school again?" she joked at his question. "Yes, I like him. He's a very kind man."

"No, Steph, you know what I mean." Will narrowed his eyes. "Do you have feelings for him? Because if you do, you have a little boy looking for a father figure. Is Julian willing to step into that role?"

"You don't think he can?" she asked.

"Not my question," he said annoyingly. "Do *you* think he'd be a good father figure?"

She didn't even hesitate. "Yes. I do."

Will just stared at her, then shrugged. "Okay."

"Okay?" she said.

"Yeah, okay."

"Why are you so angry?" She didn't understand where this hostility had suddenly come from.

"I just don't trust him a hundred percent," Will said.

"Why? He's been nothing but kind to you," she said, disappointed in her brother. He saw the changes. Julian had cleaned himself up. He was the old Jules who loved not only life, but their life in Blueberry Bay.

He shook his head. "Who is in Boston that he needed to drive through a snowstorm for?"

And the doubts suddenly flooded in her head. All the things she'd overlooked with Gabe suddenly hitting her in the face. He'd had to go out of town to visit "a friend." Weather would make him "have" to stay at a friend's house. He'd give vague details or simply not bother to tell her anything.

"I have to make breakfast for Mr. Abbott," she said. "Don't you have to get to your boat?"

Asher pulled at her sleeve. "Is Jules here?"

She shook her head.

"Bummer," he said.

"That is a bummer," Max Abbott said as he walked into the kitchen.

"Oh, Mr. Abbott," she said, stepping away from Will. "This is my brother, Will, and my son, Asher."

"Will LaBelle, it's been too long!" Max Abbott walked right up to Will and hugged him.

"It has," Will said, patting his back.

"How's the lobster business these days?" Max said with a grin.

"Great," Will said.

"Oh, that's great! Just great." Max walked to Asher and held out his hand. "Good morning, son."

Asher took his hand and said, "I'm her son."

"He knows, silly," Stephanie said in a higher voice than usual. Her anxiety made her flutter around the room. "Can I get you anything, Mr. Abbott?"

"Only an extra plate so this gentleman can join us for breakfast," he said as he held out his hand towards Will. He then turned towards Asher. "Now, what grade are you in, young man?"

"Thank you for the offer," Will said, waving at them. "But I've got to go check on my boat."

"Can you still watch Asher tonight?" she asked, hoping he hadn't forgotten.

Will looked over at Asher. "You still up for the festival?"

Asher's face lit up. "Yeah!"

"Good," Will said. "Don't fill up, because we're getting a lot of peppermint cotton candy."

"Yay!" Asher held up his arms in victory.

"They still have the Winter Festival?" Max asked Asher.

"Oh yeah!" Asher sat up on his knees.

"Sit please," Stephanie said from the stove.

Asher sat down before telling Max all about the festival. "They have rides, and cotton candy, and hot cocoa." Max held out his arms wide. "They have a huge Ferris wheel."

"I haven't gone on a Ferris wheel in a very long time," Max said.

"You haven't?" Asher's mouth opened in surprise. "You should go tonight! Can he come with us, Mommy?"

Stephanie didn't know if Asher convinced Max Abbott to go to the festival or if he really needed any pushing. He agreed right away after Asher talked about all the different attractions it now had.

"You should come for old time's sake," Stephanie said.

"You know what?" He said as he turned to Asher. "I think I will."

The rest of the day, Max seemed completely lucid. She almost felt silly thinking the worst as he played checkers with Asher.

"I'll be back after my shift," she said when Janet came to relieve her, but after spending the day with him, she felt comfortable leaving him until Julian got home. She attributed his sudden lapse of lucidity to all the traveling and the shock of seeing Corrine's decorations in the house.

But once she walked into the diner, she saw the place was empty.

"It looks like everyone went to the festival," Lindy said. "Go get Asher and enjoy the night off."

Just as she pulled up to the house, she got the call from Julian. Her heart skipped a beat as they talked and agreed to meet at the Ferris wheel.

"I'll see you soon," she said as they said goodbye, and her

stomach somersaulted at the thought of being with everyone at the festival.

She ran inside and grabbed all the winter clothes she could find for Max. "I have everything to keep you warm."

He laughed as she helped him put on his winter coat. "I'll have to get some of that peppermint cotton candy Asher kept talking about."

She wasn't sure if that would be good for a man who wore dentures, but she hadn't read anything about it in the binders.

When she pulled up to the main strip where the town gathered to see the Christmas tree lit up, he had tears in his eyes.

"Corrine used to love bringing the kids to the festival," he said once she parked. "Every year when I was senator, we'd fly up from Washington DC just to come to it." The lights of the festival reflected in his teary eyes. "She would've loved meeting you."

He opened the door, slowly exited her car, and started walking down the sidewalk toward the festivities.

"I think we should find Julian," she said, as she looked around for the Ferris wheel.

But then she saw him walking through the entrance. She waved as soon as he looked over, spotting her through the crowd.

"He's over there," she shouted to Max, who now walked through the cluster of people.

Her phone started to ring. It was Will. "Hey, where are you? I just got here."

"I'm at home," he said.

"You're at home?" she said, keeping an eye on Julian. "I thought you were coming."

"Steph, you need to come home," he said.

"Why? What's wrong?" Her heart stopped immediately.

"Gabe showed up," he said.

She looked at Julian and stopped dead in her tracks. "I'll be right there."

When she reached Julian, he took her in his arms and embraced her, holding her against him. For a split second, she felt so safe in his arms, like nothing could get to her. But a jolt of reality hit her, and she stiffened.

"Are you okay?" he asked.

She could feel all the pent-up animosity making her hands shake. "I'm sorry, but I have to go home."

"Why?" Julian asked.

"It's Gabe," she said. "He's at the house."

Julian took hold of her arm. "Let me come with you."

"Your grandfather wants to see the festival," she said, backing away. "I'm sorry, but I need to go now."

She turned around and started walking, then running toward her car, leaving Julian and Max behind. She didn't look back, just got into her car and pulled out, then drove as fast as she could with the roads being as messy as they were.

When she pulled into the driveway, she saw him in the picture window. He looked heavier than the last time she'd seen him.

"What are you doing here?" She walked straight through the house to the spot where he sat.

Both Will and her father watched him from their usual positions.

Gabe held up his hands. "I'm here to ask if I can come to Christmas."

She wrinkled her forehead in distrust. "You want to come *here* for Christmas?"

He nodded. "I want to be with you and Asher."

She shook her head, then looked for Asher. "Where is he?"

"He's upstairs watching a Christmas movie in my room," Will said. It was the quietest place in the house.

"Let's talk in the garage," she said to Gabe.

She turned and walked straight to the garage without waiting for his response, wishing she could scream or throw something at him. But instead, she crossed her arms and waited for him to come out.

"I didn't call because you were ignoring my calls," he said as soon as he shut the door, which was true.

"Did you call your lawyer?" she asked.

He shook his head.

She looked away from him as the tears stung the backs of her eyes. "All I've ever wanted was for you to be consistent for him."

"I know," he said, looking at the ground. "I'm sorry."

"But you never follow through." She shook her head.

Maybe that was her problem. Maybe that's why Will had warned her about Julian. Did she purposely choose men who couldn't be reliable?

"I have presents for him," Gabe said. "And if you don't want me to stay here, I've got my parents' place."

"You want to stay here?" Where did he get the nerve?

Gabe's head dropped. "I know I've made a mess. I'm just trying to start fixing it."

She looked into his familiar eyes. He had lied straight to her face so many times. How could she trust him? How could she trust any man?

She shivered as she stood in the garage, the bay door open to the outside, when lights reflected off the walls and then blinded her from the driveway.

"What the...?" Gabe said, covering the light with his hand.

She saw Julian's car's emblem between the lights. He turned off the car and got out.

"Who's this?" Gabe asked her as Julian walked toward her.

"Hey," he said, coming up to her. She could see Max in the passenger's side. "You okay?"

She rubbed her arms with her hands. "Yeah, just fine. What are you doing here?"

"Well, my grandfather said he didn't want to go to the festival without Asher," he said. He looked over to Gabe and held out his hand. "It's good to see you again, Gabe."

Gabe wrinkled his face like he smelled a skunk. "Who are you?"

"Gabe, this is Julian Abbott," she said, without mentioning that he was her boss.

Gabe stuck out his hand hard and awkwardly. Julian took it gracefully and comfortably.

"You've got the greatest kid, man," Julian said.

And she saw Gabe loosen up as he let go of Julian's hand.

"Thanks," Gabe said, checking out Julian. The two couldn't be more different. "What's he doing here?" Gabe asked, insecurity suddenly coming out in his voice.

"Is everyone inside?" he asked her, as he squeezed her arm just enough to make her relax. "I thought I'd bring my grandfather over, and we could all go back to the festival together." He turned to Gabe. "Did you come up for the festivities?"

Will stepped out of the house, into the garage, leaving the door open. "The festival is going to end soon. We're going without you guys."

Already in his winter gear, Asher walked out of the house in boots, a hat, and gloves. "Is that Mr. Abbott?"

Asher ran to the car waving his hands. "I'm going to the festival now!"

Max waved both of his hands just like Asher. "I am, too!"

Stephanie let out a little laugh and saw Gabe did, too.

"Wait a second," Stephanie said, holding her arm to stop him. She looked at Gabe. "Do you want to invite your dad?"

Gabe shot Asher a look, and she could see he wasn't sure if Asher would agree or not.

"Sure. You want to come, Dad?" Asher asked.

"Yeah, buddy, I'd love to," he said.

"You can meet us there," she said to Gabe. She wasn't trusting this new change, but she wouldn't keep Asher from his father.

"Let me drive," Julian said to her.

She nodded and followed him to his car. He opened the back door for her and Asher, and just before she got in, he whispered, "Are you sure you're okay?"

She nodded, "Yeah, I'm fine."

He cocked his head.

"Seriously," she said, resigned. "I just want Asher happy."

"You're a good mom," he said.

"You're a good man," she said back to him. "Thanks for coming to my rescue."

She ran over to her car and grabbed Asher's booster seat. She didn't know why Julian had come, but he had saved the moment. She would've stayed out there fighting. Asher would've missed the festival. Things would've been weird afterward. Asher would've gotten upset, and things could've escalated. But now, Asher had his whole family going to the festival.

Will got into Julian's car, too, squeezing her in between him and Asher. He reached his hand over the console to Max. "Good to see you again, Mr. Abbott."

"Good to see you, too, William," Max said.

"Where's Dad going?" Stephanie asked Will when she saw him get into his truck.

"He's meeting Bonnie," he said.

"Does Grandpa have a girlfriend?" Asher asked.

Will shrugged and Stephanie said, "Yes, I think he does."

"Do you have your shells?" Julian asked everyone.

Asher held up the large clam fan shell. "I do!"

Max held up a bag and shook it. "We brought extra!"

"Do you know about the town's tradition?" she asked Max.

"Oh, yes!" he said. "I used to make my own as a little boy."

"To the festival!" Asher called out, pointing his finger up in the air.

Julian pulled the car in reverse. "To the festival!"

It took less than five minutes to reach a parking spot down-town. When they all got out, Gabe met them and offered to pay for Asher, but when Julian pulled out his credit card and paid for everyone, Gabe stuffed his wallet back inside his jacket.

They all walked along the main strip, Gabe tried to reminisce about going with Stephanie as a teenager, but she didn't remember going with him. She did remember going with her mom and making seashell ornaments.

"Let's make the ornaments," she said to Asher.

"Yeah," he said.

"How about a ride first?" Gabe said.

Asher shook his head. "I want to do the shell first and see Santa come on his boat."

"They still do that?" Gabe said, clearly disappointed. "How about the Ferris wheel?"

"No, I want to make my ornament." Asher grabbed Stephanie's hand. "Jules, you'll make the ornaments with us, right?"

"Sure, Asher," Jules said.

Gabe's face turned red, but he didn't say anything. "Fine, then after the ornaments."

"I'll get the hot chocolate," Will said.

"Let me help you," Gabe said. "It's on me."

This made Asher jump in joy, but Stephanie had to hold back a comment.

Stephanie steered Asher to the tent where the ornaments were made, with Julian by Max's side. Max slowed them down as he shook people's hands when they recognized him.

"Merry Christmas, Senator," some said, while others joked, "We need you back in office!"

"I'm afraid I enjoy retirement too much," Max joked back, but by the time they reached the tent, he looked tired.

"Let's get you a seat," she said, pulling out a folding chair for him.

"Only if this little guy sits next to me." He patted the seat. "Come on, Steven."

Asher didn't notice the name change, but Julian did.

When they sat down, she pulled Julian back, out of earshot. "He had a few instances last night when he called me Corrine."

Worry lines deepened in Julian's forehead. "I didn't know."

She had worried about that. "I think it happens more when he gets tired."

She thought back to last night and how many times he kept referring to her as Corrine. She didn't want to worry Julian, but he should be aware of some of the things she had noticed that were of concern, like thinking she was his deceased wife.

"I'm so glad you stayed with him," Julian said, squeezing her hand.

And that's when that feeling washed over her. It made her feel like the world was spinning and made her knees wobbly. "Of course."

He kept her hand in his, and his eyes penetrated her. "I haven't stopped thinking about you."

"Oh." She didn't know how to respond.

"I missed this," he said, holding out his other hand toward Asher. "I missed both of you."

Her heart stretched like it always did when he and Asher were together.

"We've missed you, too," she said.

"I like being in Blueberry Bay with you," he said.

"You do?" She almost didn't believe him and she thought about Will's warnings. Would he stick around? Or would he bolt like Gabe?

He nodded. "I want to get to know you and Asher better."

"You do?" She covered her mouth with her free hand, but he pulled it away. "Even if my lame ex-husband shows up unannounced?"

He nodded. "All I want to do is make you and Asher happy."

She laughed, her hand trying to cover her mouth again. "You do?"

"Yes, that's all I want," he said. "And a thirty-six-foot lobster boat."

"A lobster boat? What?" she asked completely at a loss for words. Did he say he wanted a lobster boat?

"What do you think of our shell ornaments?" Asher asked, suddenly standing in between them holding two shells up.

She looked down at the shell, which had dots marking the tops of several sticks. "It's nice."

"It's all of us at Christmas," he said. He pointed to all the dots. "Me, you, Uncle Will, Grandpa, Jules, Max, and Daddy."

"That's a lot of people," Stephanie said.

"You forgot Oliver and Muriel," Julian said. "I can't have a Christmas without my brother and his wife."

"Mrs. Abbott celebrates Christmas too?" This seemed to blow Asher's mind. He looked up at Stephanie. "We'll have to make so many cookies for Santa this year."

Julian squeezed her hand. "Let me help."

"Okay," she said, keeping her hand in his.

Asher seemed pleased with his creation and tugged Max to the harbor so they could get a good look at Santa when he arrived in his boat.

Will and Gabe finally came with hot chocolate and warm fried dough just as Santa made his big entrance into the harbor.

"He's coming!" Asher screeched out. "He's coming!"

Julian held her hand in one hand, and Asher's in his other. She was exactly where she wanted to be.

Gabe took Asher to the Ferris wheel as Stephanie and Julian got cotton candy. When the festival's fireworks went off into the night, the whole town stood under their lights. Red and green and blue and white sparkles danced throughout the sky as people below made ohhs and ahhs. After the finale finished with a rapid succession of the most dazzling fireworks, they all walked back to the car.

Gabe gave Asher a big hug and waved at everyone else.

"I'd like to come by in the morning, before I head back to Portland," he said.

"Of course," she said. "You can always see your son, Gabe. Always."

He gave her a nod and left.

Julian kept her hand in his until they reached the car and only let go to open the door for her. When they got in the car, Asher leaned over and rested his head on her shoulder, making a big yawn.

"You tired?" She rubbed his face gently with her hand.

He closed her eyes. "I wish it was Christmas already."

"Just a few more days, buddy," Will said on the other side.

When Julian pulled into the driveway, Will and Asher got out and headed inside. Stephanie lagged behind as Julian followed her to the house.

"What are you doing tomorrow?" he asked when they reached the door.

"Spending time with you," she said back.

He smiled and time seemed to stop at that moment.

Maybe it was because she worried that she might not ever get another chance. Or maybe it was because he looked so handsome standing under the stars in the snow. Or maybe she just wanted to finally do something for herself, but she wrapped her arms around his neck and kissed him.

At first, he tensed up as if surprised, but then he enveloped her with his arms and kissed her so tenderly and passionately that she was breathless when they parted lips.

"Thanks for taking me to the festival," she said, stepping away.

He held her hand as she left, pulling her back to him and kissing her all over again. "Call me in the morning and I'll pick you and Asher up and we'll go on an adventure."

"What are we going to do?" she asked, playing with his fingers.

"You'll just have to wait and find out," he said and kissed her again.

She stood on the porch as he walked to his car and left. She inhaled the crisp night's air and looked up at the moon.

"I know you had something to do with tonight," she said up at the sky. Her mother was somewhere up there. "Thank you."

# CHAPTER 21

*M*ax Abbott knew he had lived a good life, and tonight was no exception. He was lucky. He had what most people strived for their whole lives. He had a great family and had been blessed to have married the most patient and wonderful woman. He'd had a fulfilling career and a large bank account to show for it. But one thing he had been especially grateful for was the house in Maine. It had been the place where the family came together. They had come to live, rest, play, love, heal, and even die in this home.

It had been a privilege he was allowed to have been the curator of the house for most of his adult life had been one of the greatest responsibilities of his life. That's why he was so certain it had to go to the right person when he was ready to leave the physical world.

He sighed as he watched the flames dance in the fireplace. He looked over to Julian.

"Steven, is your mother still decorating?" he asked.

"Gramps, it's me, Julian."

Max shook his head. "Oh, yes, Julian."

Max looked around the room again. "Your mother's always finding something new to add to her collection."

He liked teasing his wife, but he secretly loved her Christmas passion. She made the large house feel warm and cozy. Her dedication and effort during the holiday kept everyone wanting to come back to spend time together.

"You going to go to bed soon, Gramps?" Julian asked.

Max shook his head. "I think I'll stay here and watch the fire."

He really wanted to sit quietly by himself and admire Corrine's work. She always did a special tree for his lounge just for him. She chose the colored lights that reminded him of his childhood. She'd put the nutcrackers they'd gotten in Germany on the mantel and the advent calendar his grandmother had made. Some men were blessed with good fortune and some with intelligence. Max Abbott was blessed to have a wife who loved him with all her heart.

Once he was all alone, he said, "I think I'm ready."

He got up as the fire went out. He climbed the steps to his bedroom, admiring the tree as he ascended the stairs.

As he turned the light off by the bedstand he said, "Merry Christmas, my love."

And Max Abbott fell asleep dreaming of Corrine.

# CHAPTER 22

*W*hen his grandfather didn't come down for breakfast, Julian had a funny feeling that something wasn't right. Then, when Janet arrived, her reaction confirmed his fears.

"He hasn't woken up, yet?" Her face was stricken.

"I'll go upstairs," he said.

He knocked first before opening the door and then saw his grandfather lying in the bed. He was as still as could be. Slowly, Julian approached the bed, hugged his grandfather one last time before leaving to call the ambulance. Janet met Julian at the bottom of the stairs and hugged him right as he told her, crying on his shoulder. Everything felt like a blur after that.

He called his father after the ambulance came and then Oliver. But it was when he called Stephanie that his emotions finally found their way to the surface.

"Hey, good morning. I was just going to call you," she said.

"There's something I've got to tell you." He didn't want to ruin Asher's Christmas. He didn't want Stephanie to be frightened of losing her job, but the truth was, he wasn't sure what would happen now. "My grandfather passed away last night."

"Oh my gosh, I'm so sorry, Julian," she said. "Let me get Will and I'm going to come over there right away."

"No, you probably shouldn't," he said, thinking about the arrival of his family. They had taken a private flight and would be arriving at the house soon. "It's going to be pretty chaotic here. My family's coming. The press will most likely come too."

"What can I do for you?" she asked.

He didn't know. "Just be there."

"I'm here when you need me," she said.

"Stephanie," he said. "I don't know what's going to happen with your position."

"Shush," she said. "That's the last thing you need to worry about now."

But he did worry about it. He worried about it all day as more and more people came into the house and started taking over things. He felt sick when his father arrived; worse, when his mother didn't.

"Where's Mom?" he asked, sitting with Oliver, Muriel, and Janet.

"I told her to stay in New York," his father said, rattling the ice in his glass of whiskey.

"Why?" Julian didn't understand. "Wasn't she coming for Christmas?"

"Well, now we'll have to go to Boston for the funeral," he said.

"You're not having the funeral here?" Julian felt like his grandfather would've wanted that. "Is that what he wants?"

"I'm assuming he'd want to be given a decorative funeral, because he was one of the state's longest-running senators." His father typed on his phone as it began to ring. He answered. "Give ABC and the other networks a statement from the family."

Julian sat, annoyed, wondering what the statement would say.

As his father continued talking on the phone, Janet entered the room. "I've called and made the arrangements for the funeral home."

"Thanks, Janet," Steven said before walking out of the room.

"He doesn't even care that his father died," Julian said to Oliver, who sat in the lounge with Muriel.

"That's not true," Oliver said. "He just shows his emotions through action."

When his father came back in, he looked around the room. "You decorated?"

Julian nodded.

His father studied the Christmas tree. "He still had you put up these silly decorations?"

His father plucked off one of the shell decorations Julian had made with Asher.

"That's mine," Julian said.

Steven scrunched his forehead at that and returned the ornament, moving on to another.

The bell to the gate rang, and his father held out his phone to Julian. "Do you know this woman?"

Janet peeked at the screen. "That's Stephanie, the new house manager."

Steven made a face. "You ended up finding someone?"

"She's great," Janet said. "She'll be very professional during this transition."

Steven shook his head. "Has she signed anything yet?"

Janet's eyebrows wrinkled. "Um, not that I'm aware of."

"Then we'll just let her go at this point," Steven said.

Janet flashed a look at Julian.

He stood up. "You can't fire her. She just left her job to come work for us."

"Us?" Steven looked at him like he was being unreasonable. "There's no point in keeping her now that Gramps isn't here."

"You can't do that to her," Julian protested. "She needs this job."

Steven narrowed his eyes at Julian, studying him. "Who is this woman? Please tell me you're not sleeping with her."

"Dad!" He couldn't believe his father.

Janet's mouth dropped and she removed herself from the conversation. "I should get the door."

"She's a maid, Julian," he said. "Not a good look for someone trying to clean up his reputation."

"I don't care about my reputation." He had nothing but disgust for his father's attitude because that had once been his own attitude. "I care about my integrity."

"Your mother and I are not keeping the house," his father said, and Julian's worst fears had come true. "After that, she won't have a house to manage."

"Mr. Abbott?" Janet interrupted. "This is Stephanie LaBelle, the new house manager."

His father turned around to greet Stephanie. His mood completely changed once he saw what she looked like. Beauty seemed to trump social class for Steven.

"Ms. LaBelle, I appreciate all that you did for my father." He reached out his hand, smiling at her. He looked like he did when he was negotiating a deal.

"I didn't get to spend too much time with him, but he was a great man," she said.

She snuck a glance over at Julian and Steven noticed. He smirked at his son.

"I'm so sorry," she said to Julian as more family arrived, stealing Steven's attention. "How are you doing?" She stepped back and hit herself on the forehead. "That's such a stupid question. Of course you're not okay. How could you be?"

His demons whispered in his head about how nice a drink would feel. If his father could stop being such a jerk, he might have invited her to stay, but he wasn't sure what to do.

"Janet suggested I come by to help as your family arrives," Stephanie said.

"That's nice of you," he said, stepping back and making space between them before his father said something inappropriate. "But you should just go home. We'll be okay."

Just as Julian was about to lead Stephanie out, Steven approached her.

"We'll need help getting the house ready to put on the market, but I'm sure you realize, now that my father's passed, your services will no longer be needed," Steven said it as he looked down at his phone, not even giving Stephanie the courtesy of eye contact while he essentially fired her.

The whole room froze in silence as they all looked at Stephanie, who stood like a deer in headlights.

"Dad!" Julian said, raising his voice. "This is completely inappropriate."

His father looked at Stephanie "You understand, don't you? The house will be empty now. We're going to put it on the market. So, consider this your two-week's notice."

Stephanie stood there, her hands clasped in front of her, keeping her emotions in check. She straightened her shoulders and picked up her chin a bit. Julian shook with rage.

"Yes, of course." She gave him a nod. She didn't even look at Julian when she spoke. "I'm sorry for your loss, Mr. Abbott."

And she turned to leave the room when his father mumbled loud enough for everyone to hear, "She's lucky I didn't fire her for patronizing with my son."

Stephanie took off after that, speed walking out of the room.

"Stephanie!" Julian went after her. "Wait!"

But she didn't slow down, if anything she sped up, cutting through the dining room and straight to the kitchen.

"Please, wait," he said, as he caught up to her.

She stopped and turned to face him. Tears ran down her face. "It's ok, really. I should go."

"I'm so sorry," he said. He reached out to take her in his arms, but she stepped away from him. "I didn't know he would do that right then."

She shook her head. "I shouldn't make this about me. You just lost your grandfather. How are you?"

But she looked like her world had just turned upside down.

"Don't worry about the position," he said. "I'll help you find another family who will appreciate your services."

She shook her head. "You don't get it. I have a son."

"I know." He could not believe his father just said what he did.

"Lindy's already replaced me and it's not that easy to find another waitressing job." Stephanie shook her head. "I have a son to take care of."

His words came back to haunt him. He took her hands and held them. She reached out to the doorknob and twisted it. "I have to go."

"Please don't go." He could feel himself wanting to beg. He took hold of her hand, but she pulled away.

She opened the door and turned back to him. "I really am sorry about your grandfather."

And with that, she shut the door before he could reach out and stop her.

She pulled away as a news van showed up outside the house. He could hear everyone gathered in the television room. More and more of his aunts and uncles showed up, along with some of his cousins. Most acted like it was a reunion, and in some ways, it was, which made Julian even more upset. Why had they waited until his grandfather had died to get together?

"How've you been?" his aunt Joyce asked.

"Fine. I've been fine," he said, hoping the conversation would end there.

"Are you seeing anyone these days?" she asked.

"Yes, Julian, are you?" his father asked.

Julian gave his aunt a half smile, but didn't answer.

"Oh, well, there are some nice girls around my neighborhood, all with careers," she said.

"I guess he doesn't need a career if he can get a woman to support him," his father said from his chair, getting bolder with each sip of whiskey. "How much does a housekeeper make?"

Julian gritted his teeth. He would not take the bait. He

wouldn't disrespect Gramps. He had used the tools Father Michael taught him. He'd let it go. Move on.

"Aunt Debra," he turned to his aunt. "How is Florida this time of year? Gramps complained it had been awfully hot."

His aunt abandoned the inquisition about his love life and went into a story about the current state of the weather in the southeastern part of Florida.

Beside him, Oliver jabbed his elbow into his side. "Don't listen to him."

But as the afternoon wore on and the amount of alcohol consumed rose, Julian had a harder and harder time not listening to all the jabs his father took at his sons.

He texted Stephanie all day but got nothing in response.

"All that time in medical school just to become a science teacher," Steven said as their aunt Debra asked about Oliver's teaching job. Then, as he sipped his drink, he mumbled into the glass, "At least he has a job."

By the time Janet came into the room to help serve afternoon cocktails and a charcuterie board, Steven Abbott was already a few drinks in.

"Where's your girlfriend?" His father said to Julian, clearly making a joke, but Julian could feel his whole body shake inside.

"You fired her remember?" Julian said and he saw his aunts look at each other.

"You want me to just pay her to take care of an empty house?" His father mumbled something to himself.

Julian looked at his phone. No messages from Stephanie. She was avoiding him at this point. His stomach twisted at the thought of her worrying about her and Asher's future. It was all because of him, too. He had pushed her to take this job. She had a son! Janet was right all along.

"I want you to give Stephanie a severance package," he demanded to his father. "It's the right thing to do."

Steven Abbott laughed at this. "You're kidding?"

Julian shook his head. "She gave up a steady income to help Gramps. She deserves more than just a two-week notice."

His father's smile turned into a scowl. "I don't think so."

Julian wished more than anything he didn't have to do what he was about to do, but he knew it would be the only way he'd get his father to agree. "I'll go back to the company. I'll return to my job at Diversified."

His father scoffed at first, but then mulled it over. "You'll come back to the city?"

"Julian." Oliver shook his head from across the room, but the offer had already been made. He reached out his hand to his father.

Instead of taking his hand, he clapped Julian's shoulder with his fingers. "It's about time you got your senses back."

Julian swallowed down what he wanted to say. His ears ringing inside his head. What did he just do?

He stood up, unable to stay in the stuffy room any longer.

"Yeah, I have to be somewhere," he said. He stumbled backward out of the room. His father was already on his phone, not even noticing his son's whole world falling apart in front of him.

Before Julian left, he found Janet in her office. "Think you could do me a favor?"

Janet swiveled around to face him. "What's that?"

"I want you to create a severance package for Stephanie." Julian pulled up the amount on his phone.

Janet's eyes bulged out as she looked at the figure. "She's only worked here for a few weeks."

"I want her college tuition paid for," he said. If he was going to sell his soul, then he'd get her as much as he could. "She had a couple more years left at the university."

"You're father knows about this?" Janet didn't look so sure.

"Ask Oliver," Julian said, nodding his head toward the lounge where everyone gathered. "Let's just say, I made a deal he can't refuse."

Janet smiled at him and nodded. "Okay, I'll get that together for you."

"Keep in touch, okay?" he said to her.

"You're leaving?" she asked, getting out of her chair. Tears gathered on the brims of her eyes. She wrapped her arms around him and squeezed. "You, Julian, are a good grandson. Make sure you take care of yourself."

He smiled at her. "I will."

He didn't look back once he got into his car. He drove by the news vans, turning up the volume as a Christmas song played. He smiled at the thought of his grandparents back together again for Christmas and he made a turn in the direction of the toy store.

"I'm sorry I haven't picked it up yet." Julian said to Mr. Zhang.

Bryce handed over the wrapped box. "It's not a problem."

"Thank you so much for doing this for me," Julian said, shaking the toy store owner's hand.

"Anytime," he said. "Good to see you're staying in Blueberry Bay."

Julian felt a lump in his throat and couldn't correct Mr. Zhang.

"Thanks again."

When he arrived at the LaBelle's. Will met him at the door. "I'm really sorry about your grandfather."

"Thanks," Julian said, but noticed Will didn't offer him to come inside.

"Is she okay?" Julian asked.

Will nodded. "She's going to be fine."

"Come in before all the heat goes out," Brian LaBelle said from inside the house. Will stepped aside, opening the door for Julian.

"Come on in," he said.

"He was a great man," Brian LaBelle told him as he embraced Julian. Julian didn't see Stephanie.

He didn't get emotional until he saw Asher, who told him it was okay to cry.

"I did," Asher said, which made the back of Julian's throat burn.

Julian handed Asher the gift. "Do I get to open it?"

Stephanie came out from the back hallway and shook her head. "Not until Christmas."

She turned to Julian. "Help me make coffee."

Stephanie walked to the kitchen without another word. Julian followed her and sat at the table while she fixed a pot of coffee.

"I'm sorry about the position," he said.

"I shouldn't have reacted that way," she said, scooping out the grounds into the filter. "It's not your fault."

She closed the pot and turned it on. Then she sat down next to him and took his hand. "I'm okay. I'll be okay."

She gave him a smile, but it wasn't her smile. The worry still creased her forehead. He needed to get this over with before he made things even worse.

"Thanks for everything you did for Gramps over the past few days, but especially last night. He was so happy when we got home after the festival."

She smiled as the coffee brewed. "I'd like to think he was ready to let go."

Julian nodded. He felt sick to his stomach.

She sat down with two mugs and placed one in front of Julian. She put her hand on his arm. "What do you need?"

Julian reached for her hands. He didn't know how he was going to say it, so he just blurted it out. "I have to go back to the city."

"What?" Her hands jolted in his. "I thought…"

"Now that my grandfather's gone…" He looked down at the table. "I need to go back."

"But I thought you hated your job and living the city?" She looked at him as shocked as he felt.

What was he doing? Then he heard Asher in the other room and remembered why he made a deal with his father.

"Janet's going to send you a severance package for your

services," he said, getting up out of the chair. He rubbed his hands together, trying to keep his emotions at bay.

"When are you leaving?" she asked with a panic in her voice.

He shrugged, but he wasn't sure how long he could stay. "I think I'll probably head back to the city as soon as possible."

"Oh." Her eyes moistened and his heart broke. "So about Will?"

The tone in her voice switched and he hated himself for making her this upset, but this was what he had to do. He shrugged again.

"What about all that stuff about being sponsored?" She shook her head and stood up.

So, Will had told her. He lifted his hands. "Everything's changed now."

Tears filled her eyes. "And you're just going to leave?"

The lump burned in his throat, and he could barely get the word out. "Yes."

A tear fell down her cheek, but her face hardened. Her voice came out stone cold. "Make sure you say goodbye to Asher."

She pushed the chair in and walked out of the room, leaving Julian sitting in the kitchen alone.

"Where did my mom go?" Asher asked, walking into the kitchen.

Julian took a deep breath, holding his own emotions back. "She needed a minute to herself."

Asher scrunched his eyebrows and looked behind him toward where Stephanie took off.

"Can I open the gift you brought?" Asher asked, bouncing on his feet.

Julian could feel his heart being torn from his chest. "Not until Christmas."

# CHAPTER 23

*A*fter a few days, no one talked about the passing of Max Abbott except for Asher who had lots of questions.

"Did he know he was going to die?" he had asked her. "Did he hurt when he died?"

She shook her head. "I don't think so."

"Do you know when the funeral will be?" her father asked. "The news said it would be held in the cathedral in Boston next week."

"I wish Jules was here," Asher said for the millionth time. At this point, Stephanie ignored it. What else could she do?

Her father got up from his spot at the table and stood beside her at the stove and looked at what she was doing then quickly dipped his finger in the batter for her blueberry muffins.

"Get out of there." She playfully smacked his hand, and he dashed away stuffing his finger in his mouth.

"What'd you do, Grandpa?" Asher asked.

"What I always do—bother your mother." He laughed. When the doorbell rang, Stephanie didn't think anything of it until she heard Janet's voice.

She quickly wiped her hands with a dishtowel and met Janet at the front door.

"Janet?" she said, walking into the room. "What are you doing here?"

Janet held out a black binder to Stephanie and her stomach dropped. She never wanted to see a black binder again. "What is that?"

"Your severance package." Janet pushed it into her hands. "I thought we could go over some of the terms."

"There are terms?" Stephanie wasn't expecting anything from the Abbotts after she left that day. She hadn't even heard from Steven Abbott about finishing up the two weeks, not that she had planned on it. She didn't want to return to that house and see that man again.

Janet nodded. "Can we talk in private?"

Her father gestured toward the living room. "Come on, Ash, let's have a snack in the kitchen. You ladies take your time."

Stephanie let Janet sit down first, holding the binder, but didn't look inside. What kind of severance would Steven Abbott give to the help who he accused of seducing his son?

"Julian doesn't want me to tell you this, but he's the one who set up the whole package." Janet nodded at the binder with her chin. "You'll see he's been quite generous."

Stephanie set it down in front of Janet. "I don't want to accept anything from the Abbotts."

Janet closed her eyes, shaking her head. "Julian is not his father. Don't punish him for what Steven said. It was a very emotional day."

Stephanie didn't want to hold onto a grudge. From what she's heard, Steven Abbott had always acted like a donkey's rearend. It was Julian who broke her heart.

Her eyes stung at the thought of him leaving without an explanation. "He left."

"What?" Janet scrunched her forehead.

"He left for the city once his father embarrassed him for dating the help." Stephanie didn't think Julian had been that shallow, but the facts were the facts. Julian stopped seeing her the minute his father reared his ugly head.

"That's not the reason he went back." Janet crossed her legs. "Open the dang binder."

Stephanie put it on the coffee table. "I don't want anything from the family."

Janet huffed, standing up and opened the cover, then flipped through to a section marked with a florescent pink tab.

"The University of Maine?" Stephanie said, reading the letter-head. "What's this?"

"Turn the page." Janet sighed. She wasn't going to just tell Stephanie.

Stephanie waited as long as she could before relenting and opening the cover. "Tuition Agreement?"

"Yes. He'll pay for you to finish your degree," Janet said smiling at her. "And, there's a position at the registrars' office that you can work at while taking classes."

"What?" Stephanie couldn't believe it. "This is my severance?"

"Julian pulled a lot of strings," Janet said.

Stephanie closed the cover and pushed it across the table back to Janet. "Thank you, but I'm not going to accept this."

"Why?" Janet looked baffled.

"Because, this is just a pity present." Stephanie shook her head. "I want nothing to do with it."

Janet sat there staring at Stephanie for an uncomfortable minute before saying, "He sacrificed his happiness for you."

Stephanie watched Janet, confused, as she stood up, leaving the binder on the table.

"He went back to work for his father to get this for you." Janet zippered up her coat. "I'm looking forward to Florida, but I'm going to miss the Abbotts. They have always been very good to me."

Stephanie didn't know what to say, but pulling strings wasn't what she had wanted or needed. "I thought he loved me."

Janet let out a laugh. "He loves you so much he was willing to let you go."

She walked toward the door.

"Take a look at the binder," Janet said. "Let me know if you have any more questions."

Janet let herself out as Stephanie stared at the black book. She didn't know what to do. It was easier to be mad at him. Easier to think that he chose to leave and go back to work for himself, not for her.

She flipped open the cover and began reading through. The whole binder had been clearly written by someone who handled contracts with tons of legal jargon, but the summary clarified that Stephanie could finish her degree from the University she had previously attended, fully funded by Steven Abbott.

"Is he still in Blueberry Bay?" she asked. She had to see him. What was he thinking making a deal like this?

Janet shook her head. "They all went back to the city."

Stephanie grabbed the binder and opened it. "He went back to work for his father? Why would he do that?"

Janet looked at her like she was crazy.

"Because he's in love with you!" Will said from the back hallway.

Stephanie twisted around to see her brother and father eaves-dropping. "I have to go to the city."

She stood up and looked at her dad. "Can you take care of Asher?"

"Don't get a speeding ticket," her father warned her.

She ran over to her father and hugged him. "I'll be careful!"

She grabbed her purse and started running around the room, trying to collect everything she needed, but she had no idea where she was really going or what she was about to do. "Where should I go first?"

"Let me drive you," Will said, taking his coat out of the closet.

"Really?" Stephanie smiled at her brother.

"You're a maniac on the road." Will said, grabbing the keys to her car. "We'll take yours. Better on gas."

Asher gave her a big hug when she told him the plan. "Listen to Grandpa."

"I will," he said, playing with his Transformers.

"Let's go!" Will shouted out from the back door.

She kissed Asher one last time and ran out the door.

The drive took exactly five hours. Five of the most anxiety-ridden hours of her life. What if Janet was wrong about Julian's intentions?

By the time they reached the city, it was past six. "Do you think he's still at work?"

Will leaned close to the windshield, looking at the street signs. "I think it's time we text him."

She shook her head. "I need to see his face. I need to know this is what he wants to do."

"Ok, but we need to first figure out where he is?" Will honked his horn. "No one uses a blinker here."

She opened her phone and typed *Julian Abbott* into the search bar. Images of Julian popped up on the screen. A profile shot of him in a three-piece suit with a job description underneath, Julian Abbott, Financial Loan Officer, Diversified Business and Credit.

She called his office's number.

A woman's voice answered, "Diversified Business and Credit, how can I direct your call?"

"Yes, hi, I'm wondering if Julian Abbott is still in the building?" she asked.

"Yes, Mr. Abbott is still here," the woman answered. "Would you like me to put you through to his office?"

Stephanie hung up. "He's still there. Head to his office, it's just around the corner."

"Why'd you hang up?" he asked as they parked in the garage across the street. "Why didn't you tell him you're here."

She didn't know why, but she was nervous. She had never made a grand gesture before. "I don't know—just come with me."

She opened the glass doors to the skyscraper and looked up into the tall glass lobby. Men and women rushed by her in dark suits, clicking their heels against the marble floors and talking into devices. Everyone seemed busy and important. No one even noticed them.

She walked up to the information desk. "Excuse me?" She said to a man reading from his phone. "Which floor is Diversified Business and Credit?"

"Floor thirty-one," the man said pointing to the elevator.

"Thank you," Stephanie called out as she rushed to hit the button to go up. She looked behind her to Will hanging back. "Aren't you coming up?"

He shook his head. "No, I think I'm going to let you talk to him on your own."

She almost protested but stopped herself. "Thank you for coming with me."

"No problem," Will said.

He didn't do well with emotional stuff, so she had to keep it light. "I've missed this."

"Missed what?" he asked.

"Missed us hanging out and doing stuff together," she said. "I always loved being your sister, but I've missed being your friend."

Ever since Asher had been born, their relationship hadn't been the same. Maybe it was her, maybe him, probably both of them, but when their mother died, their relationship drifted even further apart.

He nodded. "I've missed hanging out, too."

She smiled at him as the elevator dinged. "I'll be back."

"Tell Julian to just come home," Will said as she stepped into the elevator.

She waved as she hit the button for the thirty-first-floor and the doors closed.

The ride up felt like the longest elevator ride in her life and her head started racing through every doubt she had. Would he even want to come back to Blueberry Bay?

When the doors opened she almost hadn't noticed, she was so wrapped up in her thoughts, but then she saw a woman behind a desk with big letters written behind, spelling, *Diversified Business and Credit.*

"May I help you?" she asked, but she almost looked disturbed by Stephanie's presence. "Office hours are nine to five-thirty."

"Yes, I'm sorry," Stephaie said, "I'm looking for Julian Abbott."

"Regarding?" the woman asked, as she picked up her phone's receiver.

She was thrown off. What did she say? Regarding her severance?

"Lobsters," she blurted out.

The women's eyebrows lifted. "Lobsters?"

"Yes. Lobsters," Stephanie spoke more confidently, but she wrung her hands.

"Let me tell him you're here about lobsters." The woman punched a button and adjusted the phone. "Yes, I have a woman here to see you about lobsters?"

She kept her eye on Stephanie, suspiciously. Then she covered the mouthpiece. "And your name is...?"

"Stephanie?" Julian walked down the hallway to the front lobby. "What are you doing here?"

"Honestly?" She looked at the secretary whose full attention was now on them. "I can't accept the severance package."

His face dropped. "Why not?"

"Because I can't ask you to do this for me." She flung her arms out at the lobby's walls. "I don't need a fancy job title or a fancy degree. Not at the expense of your happiness."

Julian shook his head. "I made you take the position."

"No one makes me do anything," Stephanie said, shaking her head. "Like taking this terrible severance package. Tell your dad, I won't accept it."

"Stephanie, come on, you have Asher to think about." Julian's voice sounded defeated.

"I am thinking of Asher," she said. "He's been miserable without you around."

Julian shook his head. "He's got his father."

"He needs you, too." She shook her head, walking up to him. "And…" She didn't care if she looked like a fool in front of the secretary or a gold digger to his father or what anyone else thought. "I need you."

She wanted him to run to her. Take her in his arms and whisk her into a kiss. But all Julian did was stand there.

"Take my father's offer," he said. "It's done."

His shoulders fell as he looked at her.

"It's not done," she said, rushing over to him. She grabbed hold of his arm. "I won't take the money."

Julian frowned. "You need to. Please, this is how I can make things right."

"Julian, please," she was begging at this point. "Look at me. Tell me you really want to stay here and work with your dad."

The look in his eyes said it all and crushed her heart. He was broken.

"I know you, Julian," she said. "You don't belong here."

Stephanie didn't know when she stopped fighting for what she wanted in life. She couldn't blame Gabe or the expectancy of Asher. Why did she stop? What made her feel like she couldn't get more out of life.

"I love you," she said. "I love you and I want us to be together."

She played with her nails as he stood there. His secretary watched them like it was a motion picture film.

He didn't move or say anything at first. Then his eyes watered. "It's too late."

Just as Julian was about to turn around, the elevator dinged and Will walked out. He could sense the discussion wasn't going well by the look of desperation on Stephanie's face.

"Julian!" Will said. "Come fish lobsters with me."

"So, this *is* about lobsters?" the secretary laughed.

"I can't," Julian shook his head. "I have an apartment here and a job."

"You can stay with us until you figure things out," Will said, as Stephanie nodded furiously.

"You can take my room, and I stay with Asher," she said, praying he'd reconsider.

"I need to go back to work," Julian said, not moving from his spot. "I'm sorry you drove all this way for nothing."

"Julian." Her throat dried up as he started to walk away.

Will walked to her side. "Let's go."

"Wow, I can't believe he just walked away," the secretary whispered out loud to herself.

Stephanie couldn't believe it, either.

# CHAPTER 24

*C*hristmas Eve had always started with preparing the fish right away. Even her father and brother would help Stephanie and her mother in the kitchen…until the games came on. But for a few good hours, just the four of them would work together to make the seven-fishes dinner, their family's traditional Christmas Eve meal.

As a child, Stephanie loved it. As an adult and mother, she had dreaded being in charge of the full-days' worth of cooking. When she took over the meal after her mother had died, it was up to her to do everything and the boys, in their grief, were happy to leave it up to her, because they didn't care one way or the other. But she cared because she wanted Asher to have those same memories.

This year, with the passing of Max Abbott and Julian leaving, she promised herself to make this the best holiday for Asher.

So, at four AM, she dragged herself out of bed and headed to the kitchen. Turning on the light, she jumped when she saw her father sitting in the dark with a cup of coffee.

"Dad!" she cried out. "What are you doing?"

"I'm always up this early," he said. "I was waiting for you to get up."

"You don't want to sleep in?" she asked.

He shook his head. "I haven't slept in for thirty years."

She walked over to the coffee maker and poured herself a cup. "I guess all those years fishing will do that to you."

He got up and rolled his sleeves up. "How can I help?"

She scrunched her eyebrows together. "You want to help?"

"It's Christmas Eve," he said. "I always used to help."

"Not since mom died," she said it before she could take it back and she could see the sting.

"Hmmm." He looked out the window at the blackness. "You just took over and never seemed to want my help. You were always so independent. Just like your mother. We only got to help out because Will wanted to be with you and mom."

Stephanie thought back to all those Christmas Eves. She didn't remember it that way. "I would really love your help today."

He gave her a nod. "I'd really love to help."

She smiled as he pulled out the octopus. "Did you get this from Emil?"

The local fish market had everything. "Yup."

"When's the twit coming?"

"Gabe's going to come for dinner on Christmas Eve and then again on Christmas for presents," she said, stuffing the chicken like her mother used to do. "I've told you this multiple times."

Her father huffed. "Well, I still can't believe he's coming."

"It's about Asher, Dad," she said. But it was more than just Asher. It was about opening her heart to change. If she stayed stuck and angry at Gabe, that anger would permeate other areas of her life. She couldn't afford that.

"Fine, but I don't have to like it."

Footsteps were heard coming down the staircase and Will appeared at the bottom of the stairs.

"What are you doing up?" he asked.

"I'm making dinner," she said.

"But why this early?" Will said, opening the fridge and typing on his phone. "You're not usually up this early."

"Should I not be up?" she asked, not sure what Will's point was.

"No, it's fine." His focus went to his phone. "I'll help in a few minutes. I just have to do something."

Stephanie looked at the clock. "At four-o-six in the morning?"

"Yeah."

Will looked at her father who appeared as perplexed as she felt. His face twisted watching Will grab his coat and head to the door.

"Where are you going?" she asked him.

"Ah..." Will opened the door and looked around the yard. "No where."

He shut the door behind him. She looked at her father. "What's with him?"

He shook his head. "Beats me."

She didn't know what was going on with her brother, but she had fish to clean.

It took only an hour to clean them all. She had lobster, muscles, cod, scallops, and more.

"You're doing the sardines still?" her father wrinkled his nose as she took out the small, silvery fish.

"You used to love the sardines," she said.

"I pretended, for your mother's sake, but I never really liked them." He shook his head.

This made her heart warm.

"Did you invite Bonnie?" she asked.

He nodded. "She's coming at four."

"Good," she said. "It's time we get to know her."

She had to allow her father to move on, even if she didn't want him to.

He gave her a little pat on the back as he walked by her to get a knife. "I'll cut up the calamari."

She heard footsteps in the snow outside. "What is Will doing?"

Her father shrugged. "Oh, I don't know."

Suddenly, the whole yard lit up.

"What the heck?" Stephanie dropped the cod into the batter and walked to the sliding glass doors. Every tree in her yard lit up with hundreds of twinkling white Christmas lights.

She couldn't believe it. "Dad! Look outside!"

She looked at her father and noticed he was holding her coat. "It's time for your Christmas present."

"What?"

He nodded toward the front of the house and that's when she saw someone standing on the porch. She walked to the door and opened it to see Julian standing in a big winter coat and boots.

"Julian," she said. "What are you doing here?"

That's when she saw Asher coming into the hallway with Will and her father.

"What is going on?" She stepped out on the porch looking around. "When did you do this?"

"All morning," he said. "With Will."

Lights wrapped the tree trunks and individual branches. Even the smallest bush or the thinnest tree had lights covering them.

"I've never been happier than when I was with you," Julian said. The whole outside glowed with lights. "You and Asher. You make me happy."

"You need to put boots on!" she heard Asher say from inside.

She looked down at her feet in socks. "I'll be right back."

She ran to the closet when she noticed Asher holding up her boots. "Here you go, Mommy."

"Thanks, Baby," She put them on and met Julian outside.

Closing the door behind her, he took her hand and walked her off the porch and down the walkway until they were in the middle of the lights. Then, like a fairy tale, Julian got down on one knee.

"Stephanie LaBelle, would you spend the rest of your life with me?" He then took out a black velvet box and opened it up. A deep sapphire stone framed in dazzling diamond accents. It was the most beautiful ring she'd ever seen.

"Julian, this is too much," she said.

"You didn't answer the question," he said, still knelt.

She put the ring on her finger. "Yes! I say yes!"

He stood and wrapped his arms around her, dipping her into a kiss, creating a scene that she could only imagine in her dreams.

When he brought her back up, he kept her in his embrace with one arm and held out his other. "She said yes!"

Asher cheered as he ran out of the house and straight into their arms. Will and her father followed behind him, all without boots, to congratulate them. Everyone hugged Stephanie and Julian, and Asher who jumped into Julian's arms.

Julian carried Asher as they all went inside.

"We have to finish the fish!" she exclaimed, she went to rush inside, but Julian slowed her down, pulling her into his arms again. Her eye caught the ring and she stopped before going into the house to take in the moment.

"We're engaged," she laughed putting her head into his chest, admiring the beautiful blue.

"I picked it because it's as blue as a blueberry," he said. "And that's where my heart is, with you."

She shut the door, leaving them alone outside as the sun rose above the trees and she kissed him, long and passionately.

# CHAPTER 25

*A*s Stephanie stood in the kitchen she looked into the living room at Julian, who held the Lego set still as Asher fastened a brick into place. She looked down at her ring once again, feeling that tingling sensation of excitement. Her life was about to change and she and Asher were going to get their happily-ever-after.

"Have you started filling out those applications?" Will asked from the refrigerator as he peeked into the living room.

"Get out of there," she scolded. "Dinner will be ready in a half hour."

"But I'm hungry," he whined.

"Yes, I filled them out," she said, stirring the clam chowder.

"Ugh, you cooked anchovies?" He made a face.

"They're sardines," she corrected him. "Did anyone like these besides mom?"

"I don't even think your mother liked them," her dad said.

"Then why do we cook them?" she asked, looking at her mother's recipe book. Sardines were listed first on the list.

Will checked over his shoulder, seeing Julian in the other room. "I'm happy for you guys," he told her.

"I thought you said to watch out for him," she teased, poking her brother in the belly.

He shrugged. "I guess I was wrong."

"Wow, that must've been hard to admit." She put a lid on the potatoes making sure no one snuck any before dinner.

The doorbell rang, and she arranged the new dish towels nicely on their hangers.

She walked out of the kitchen and to the front door.

There, holding a tray of cookies, stood Bonnie. "Thank you so much for including me." She passed over the plate to Stephanie. "This is for you."

Stephanie took the plate and held out her hand. "It's a real pleasure to finally meet you."

She noticed her father fidgeting with his hands and brushing his hair in place. He looked nervous. She found it very cute.

"Yes, it is," Bonnie said, coming into the house.

Just as they closed the door, Gabe pulled up to the house. Asher ran out the door and jumped into his arms. "Guess what?! Mom and Jules are getting married!"

Stephanie winced as Asher told the story of Julian proposing. She didn't want Gabe to be blindsided. "Come in before you catch a cold," she said to them.

"That's an old wives' tale," Gabe said as he entered. "I guess congratulations are in order."

He stood awkwardly holding a bag of gifts. Then handed her a small one. "It's an engagement gift."

She turned the gift in her hands, checking it out. "You knew about the engagement?"

Julian walked up to Gabe and shook his hand. "Hello, Gabe. Thanks for taking my call and talking with me."

Gabe nodded. "I just want them to be happy." Gabe took off his boots. "Hello, Brian. Will." He stopped when he got to Bonnie.

"Bonnie," she said, placing her hand on her chest.

"Bonnie." He gave a nod as silence filled the room.

She would be lying if she said she didn't want Gabe to suffer a little bit, but she thought about Julian and his father. How distant their relationship had become over the years. She didn't ever want Asher to worry about that. Gabe may be a twit, but he loved his son.

"Well, let's eat!" Stephanie called out.

"Yay!" Asher jumped up and ran to the dining room.

Dinner was a success; even some of the sardines were eaten. It turned out Bonnie was a delight to talk to and seemed to really care about her dad. The two enjoyed each other, telling stories about their bowling league and laughing at each other's jokes.

"Your dad seems really happy," Julian said as they cleaned up after dessert.

She looked back in the living room, where Asher was looking through the wrapped presents under the tree to find one to open —a LaBelle family tradition since she was a kid. He dug through the boxes, looking for something in particular.

"Be careful, buddy," Will said as he moved a bigger box aside. "What are you looking for?"

When he saw Julian's gift, he picked it up and pulled it away from the rest. "This is the one I want to open."

"Okay," Gabe said. "Let's see what it is."

"Wait, wait," Stephanie called out, holding up her phone.

Asher waited for her to return to the living room and when she turned on her camera, he began to tear off the wrapping paper. "It's an Evolution Commander Armada Transformer!"

Asher ran to Julian and wrapped his arms around him, giving him a big hug. "Thank you so much, Jules!"

"Of course," Julian said.

Stephanie's heart expanded as she watched Julian show Asher how to open the transformer machine into its robot. She was sure her mother was watching over them at that moment, because it was perfect. Bonnie and her dad discussed past Christmas festivals while Will and Gabe watched the basketball game together. Tomorrow, they were invited for dinner at Muriel and Oliver's place, and they had a boat trip planned for the afternoon.

Julian got up from the couch and walked by her, grabbing her hand and pulling her into the kitchen.

"Everything okay?" she asked, still worried it was too weird to have Gabe here.

"It's perfect," he said, grabbing her jacket. He opened it up and held it out for her to put on.

"What's going on?" she said as she put her arms into the sleeves.

"Don't you want to open your Christmas present?" he asked, opening the door to the porch and holding out his hand.

She smiled, stepping outside. "A present? You already got me this ring?"

He walked to the porch swing and picked up a box she hadn't noticed before. "What did you do?"

He handed it over, and she almost dropped it because of the weight. "It's heavy." Then she said, "Don't tell me it's another binder."

She set it on the small table and sat down on the swing to open it. Julian had a huge grin across his face.

She opened the paper to reveal a box. Lifting the top, she found a large black binder like the ones Janet had given her. She looked at Julian, confused.

He opened the cover. "It's a catalog for colleges."

"What?" she asked.

"I want you to finish your college education," he said.

"What?" she asked again. She couldn't believe it. "But you left your father's company. There's no way he'll pay for this."

"This is my money," he said. "Gramps left me with a little something. Enough for you and me to buy a boat and help you finish your degree. You deserve to finish. And when you do, we can start the rest of our lives together."

"But I can't just take your money," she said, shaking her head. "It's too much."

"I love you, Stephanie, and I want to make you happy," he said. "And I know you've wanted to do this your whole life. It's time you got to finish school."

She dropped the catalog, wrapped her arms around Julian, and kissed him under the twinkling lights.

"They're kissing!" she heard Asher cheering from inside. "Eww!"

She began to laugh and pressed her head against Julian's. "We should go inside."

"One more kiss," he said and pulled her into his arms.

# CHAPTER 26

*A* lot can happen in a year. For starters, Asher was the one who calmed Stephanie down before going to school.

"But it's just so scary," she told Asher and Julian in the kitchen. "I don't want to go."

"You're going to be fine, Mom," Asher said, placating her by putting his hand on her shoulder. "I thought you liked school?"

"I do," she said. The irony of the role reversal hadn't been lost on her. "I just don't think I belong at *that* kind of school."

"It's not even an Ivy leaguer," Will said from the breakfast table.

"It's considered a Little Ivy," she snapped at her brother. "Don't you have your own house to eat at?"

The other obvious change was her and Julian's new home, just a block away from her father's place. They moved out and Bonnie moved in, prompting Will to move out and onto his new boat. Even though the new boat had a cabin with a full stocked kitchen, Will somehow always managed to end up at her breakfast table.

"I'm waiting for my sternman so we can go to work," he grumbled, stuffing a bagel into his mouth.

Julian ignored Will. "You're going to be just fine."

"But what about the Christmas Ball?" she said. "You have so much to do!"

"Janet's helping me, remember? Besides, it's my mom and dad's ball now, so all we have to do is show up," Julian assured her. "Everything is going to be just fine. Go and have fun. This is the opportunity of a lifetime."

In one of Stephanie's classes at the local university, she had been hand-selected for a special program at Bowdoin College. During the school's Christmas break, she'd have to stay three nights away from home.

"What if you guys need me?" she asked.

"We're going to be fine," Julian said. "We have plenty of people around. Plus, Bonnie and your dad are taking Asher to the movies tomorrow night."

She looked around the room, checking her bags and wondering what she had forgotten.

"I'm going to forget something; I just know it," she said, stalling to leave.

"You're going to be just fine, Mom," Asher said, packing his stuff up for school.

"Do you want me to drive you and your friends to school?" she asked. A few inches of snow had fallen on the ground.

Asher shook his head. "No, we're going to walk today."

"Okay," she said, realizing she missed another milestone. "When did you start walking to school?"

She looked at Julian, who handled the morning routine.

"We've been walking for a few weeks now," Asher answered.

"They like to play in the snow," Julian said, handing her a lunchbox. "You're going to have the best time."

She wasn't so sure. "But I'm going to miss you all."

She didn't want to leave.

Asher walked over to her and hugged her. Julian then wrapped his arms around both of them. She was exactly where she wanted to be.

"Now go become a doctor!" Asher said as he let go.

"You're walking with Zack and other older boys, right?" she asked as Asher put on his coat.

"Yup," he said.

"And you'll text us as soon as you get to school?" she asked.

"Yes, Mom," he said.

She could feel her anxiety rise, and that's when Julian took her hand, and she instantly calmed down.

"Do you want me to drive you there?" Julian asked her. "We can skip going out today. We don't need to fish."

Will sat up at that. "Seriously? She's being a baby."

Julian smiled when she made a face at her brother. She shook her head. "No, I'll be fine."

She grabbed the lunch box and zipped up her coat. "I guess it's time for me to go."

Julian followed her out to her car in his socks.

"You don't have boots on," she said, shaking her head.

He looked down, then swept her up in his arms, dipped her down into a kiss, and lifted her off her feet. When they came back up, he stared into her eyes.

"Good luck at school," he said.

"Good luck fishing," she said back to him.

"I'll see you at the ball," he told her.

She looked out across the bay to the big white house she had dreamt of living in one day—all lit up. She remembered how she'd felt a year ago, how lost and alone she'd been. Now she was grateful for the life she had.

She kissed Julian goodbye a little longer than usual, got into her car, and said, "I'll see you at the ball."

# BLUEBERRY BAY EPILOGUE

When Muriel came to Meredith about the ball, she knew exactly who would want to volunteer their time and effort to organize a community Christmas Ball. The Queen Bees.

"There hasn't been a ball at the Abbott house in over twenty-five years!" Ginny said, as they made dozens of blueberry pies for the event. She shook her head. "Such a shame, too. It was always one of the town's favorite events."

"Muriel says Steven Abbott wanted to revive the tradition," Meredith said, placing the pie crusts next to the stove.

"Did you hear that carpet bagger is now running for Senate?" Ginny rolled her eyes. "I guess he's claimed permanent residency here in Blueberry Bay."

Meredith smiled but didn't say anything about her daughter's in-laws. What would be the point? She didn't like Steven Abbott much either, but what he did or didn't do was none of her business. But she had seen a big change in the man since his father died. She would like to think it had something to do with alienating both of his sons, but it was more likely related to a senate seat opening up in his vacation state.

"It's going to be a beautiful event," Meredith said, thinking of the extravagant house perched on top of the cliffs of the Atlantic

Ocean. She couldn't wait. She felt like a teenager headed to the prom. She bought a fancy new dress and a suit for Quinn. He even joked about bringing her a corsage. She kind of hoped he would. "It's going to be so much fun with everyone there."

Even children were invited to the event, which would include a visit from Santa as part of the celebration. The whole town had been talking about the ball for weeks since the official invitations went out to each and every home in Blueberry Bay.

"Do you think the whole town will show up?" Meredith asked, trying to imagine if the Abbott house could fit everyone.

Ginny shook her head. "There are always those who'd rather not mingle with people like the Abbotts, but there's a lot of us who just like to have a good time together, no matter who you are."

Meredith smiled at Ginny. She thought back over the past years living in Maine. "I'm so glad you opened up your heart to me."

"You're one of us!" Ginny bumped her hip into Meredith's as she stirred the blueberry filling on the stove.

"There's a sculpture Jacob made of my mother in the Abbott garden," Meredith said. "I guess it's one of the first pieces he sold. She's absolutely beautiful. So young and free."

Ginny nodded. "I think I've seen it."

"I feel like that person now." Meredith could feel herself getting choked up, but she couldn't stop what she started. "I don't know what I would've done without you all."

Ginny stopped stirring and grabbed Meredith, and the two best friends held each other for a long time.

"To be honest, Meredith," Ginny said as they parted. "You were what was missing from this town. You came here and opened up your land and your heart to us. We're the ones who should be thankful."

Meredith didn't see it that way, but she felt the love of all the people around her and that was more than she could've ever asked for when she first arrived in Blueberry Bay.

When the filling was ready, they poured it into the crusts, then carefully placed the lattice lid over the fillings, and pinched the edges together gently with their fingers.

"I better start getting ready before everyone arrives here." Meredith looked down at her apron, dirty with flour. She ran up the stairs to the cottage to her new master bedroom. She had renovated it that past year to get ready for the big day when she and Quinn tied the knot. They planned a New Year's Eve wedding so they could start the year as a couple.

By the time she showered and put on her make-up, her father, Gordon, had come home from a visit with his great-grandchildren over at Remy's house.

"I can't believe Sadie is talking about colleges," he said as he made himself a cup of tea. "She's done so well in high school."

Meredith nodded. Her young niece had overcome obstacles she could never imagine and was now at the top of her class. "I'm not surprised. She was always a very smart young woman."

"And the way she is with her brother." Gordon's eyes showed his pride. "I guess she's going to the ball with her boyfriend."

"Oh," Meredith smiled. "How does Colby feel about that?"

Gordon laughed. "He's being his usual overprotective self."

Meredith chuckled. "You better get ready. We're leaving once Muriel comes with the baby."

Her latest obsession, her granddaughter, Jacqueline.

Gordon took a sip of his tea and dashed off to get ready. "I'll be ready in no time!"

Meredith stood in the kitchen in her robe, wondering if she should just put her dress on then or wait, when the back door opened and Quinn stepped inside.

Donned in a navy suit, Quinn never looked more handsome.

"Wow," he said. "You look incredible."

"So do you." She couldn't help smiling. "This isn't my dress. It's my robe."

Quinn wrapped his arms around her, kissing her as he held her against him. "You look great in everything."

She kissed him again when she heard a car pull up. "Oh, it's Cora. She and Brandon are driving with us. We'll take Muriel's car with the car seat when Jackie needs to go to bed."

"And we're staying at Muriel's?" Quinn asked.

"The plan is that when Jackie gets fussy, we'll leave with her, and let the kids have fun at the ball," she said. She wanted her daughters to have a nice time with everyone and Muriel and Oliver to have a night out and not have to worry about the baby for one night.

"Mom," Muriel said as she walked in the house holding a diaper bag. "Why aren't you ready?"

Oliver walked in with Jackie and didn't even wait for Meredith to ask for her, just passed his daughter to her grandmother.

"You got so big overnight!" Meredith squeezed her grandbaby in her arms, kissing her cheek. This made baby Jackie roll in giggles, so Meredith kissed her some more.

"Mom," Muriel said. "You need to get dressed."

"Oh yes!" Meredith passed Jackie back to Oliver and headed upstairs. "I'll be just a minute."

Meredith listened as Kyle and his girlfriend came to the house with Cora and Brandon behind them. As she came downstairs, she peeked into the living room and her whole new family gathered around her beautiful baby granddaughter. All of them celebrating together under her mother's portrait. She wanted to capture this moment and make it last forever.

"Mom's ready!" Cora called out as soon as she saw Meredith.

Meredith didn't move, just watched as everyone interacted with the baby near the lit-up Christmas tree and the hung stockings. This had been the kind of holiday she had always wanted. A family gathered together. A community that cared about its residents and wanted to help one another. And a night to look forward to, with everyone included. She couldn't believe this was her life.

Everyone filed out of the house and into their cars.

"It almost seems silly to drive since it's just down the beach," Meredith said, strapping her seatbelt in.

"You want to walk in heels on the beach?" Muriel asked from the front seat.

Meredith hadn't worn heels in some time, but she supposed it would be a bad idea. "I heard there's going to be a bonfire outside."

"It's going to be quite an event," Oliver said as he started the car. "Julian and Stephanie really did a nice job following my grandparent's traditions."

The baby spit out her pacifier and immediately began to fuss. Meredith recovered it by her foot and handed it back. She patted down the layers of tulle from Jackie's Christmas dress so she could see her grandbaby. Jackie kicked her little feet out with her patent leather shoes and Meredith had all she could do to not kiss her all over. Instead, she took her foot and pretended to eat it, which made baby Jackie fall into a fit of giggles.

"Is Nana eating your foot?" Gordon asked Jackie. "Did she eat your foot?"

"I can't help you, baby girl," Muriel said. "Your grandparents are crazy about you."

Just as they pulled into the Abbott driveway, snow began to fall. She looked out at the large colonial house all decorated with lights and garland. Each window had a candle lit in it. Wreaths hung on the doors, pine garland had been wrapped around the porch railings, and seashells placed with big gold bows. The house looked like a winter wonderland.

As they walked up the path to the house, two men dressed like nutcracker soldiers opened the front doors for them. Meredith gasped as they walked into the Abbott's front hall. Carolers and a string quartet were set up under the large spiral staircase next to the tallest Christmas tree Meredith had ever seen. People dressed as elves carried trays with appetizers and mugs of hot cocoa.

"Santa will be here in twenty minutes!" Janet called out to the crowd. "The toy workshop is in the lounge with Mr. Zhang."

"You all made it!" Genevieve Abbott said as she saw her son Oliver walk in with the others.

Genevieve kissed everyone on the cheek three times like a true Parisian woman. Meredith always felt a little unsophisticated around Oliver's mother, but she enjoyed her company. The former ballet dancer had incredible stories to tell and always looked impeccable. But Meredith also felt a little sorry for her. She was married to Steven Abbott, after all. The man almost ruined her relationship with her sons by being more worried about his bottom line than their happiness. She didn't see why anyone would stay married to a man like Steven Abbott, but that was none of her business.

That's what Meredith had learned the most about herself while living in Blueberry Bay. To not worry about the little things, like other people's relationships or how people choose to live their lives. She needed to give and love and cherish life, because it could be gone within a heartbeat.

Remy and her family arrived just before Santa. Although Remy had mentioned her son, Matthew, might not be much of a believer these days, asking more and more questions about how Santa can make it around the world in twenty-four hours.

"He's so suspicious lately that mom's been hiding the gifts at Ginny's house because she's afraid he'll find them at your mom's place," Sadie explained to Cora.

Cora laughed at her Aunt Remy. "If she runs out of room, she can always hide stuff at our place or my shop. Did you see Mrs. Abbott's linens?"

Meredith looked at the table in the dining room. A gorgeous red linen tablecloth with a decorative edging covered the table.

"Cora, it's stunning," she said, walking over to touch it. She rubbed the soft linen between her fingers. Food of all sorts covered the long table that could seat at least two dozen people. Lots of specialty treats like chocolate covered truffles and peppermint bark, along with Meredith and Ginny's blueberry pies.

"The Abbotts have always been one of my most loyal customers." Cora nodded at Janet.

As Santa passed out gifts from the North Pole, Meredith snuck her coat and approached Genevieve. "Do you mind if I check out the mermaid sculpture in the garden?"

Meredith had asked Genevieve at Jackie's baptism.

"Of course," Genevieve said in her thick French accent. "Be careful. It's a bit slippery out there with the snow."

Meredith nodded, sneaking out before she needed to take Jackie back home. Genevieve pointed to the set of French doors at the end of the front hall.

She stepped beside Quinn, who was talking with Brian LaBelle and Gordon about their bowling league.

"I'll be right back." She gestured her head toward the doors. "I'm going to check out my dad's sculpture."

"Do you want me to come with you?" Quinn asked.

She shook her head. She had actually had wanted to be alone when she saw it. "No thanks. I'm good."

The second she stepped outside the cold air hit her and she took in a deep breath. The salty tang relaxed her immediately. She listened as the waves lapped against the shore. As snowflakes fell, she carefully walked down to the Abbott garden, all lit up with Christmas lights, to Jacob's bronze sculpture.

Snowflakes fell and rested on her mother's mermaid head and shoulders and tail. This is what Meredith imagined her mother looked like in heaven.

"I hope you two are together," she said, quietly. She didn't want to hurt Gordon's feelings, but the idea that her mother was with Jacob in heaven made her loss feel a little easier. She placed her hand on her mother's bronze hand, allowing the cold to sting her skin. "I miss you so much."

She stopped talking, feeling the tears gathering behind her eyes. Looking up at the sky, she closed her eyes and listened to the waves.

"Thank you for everything," she said to Jacob. "Thank you for this wonderful life."

She didn't move for a while, and her hand was still on her mother's when Quinn came outside looking for her.

"Muriel says Jackie's getting fussy," Quinn said.

"Okay," Meredith said. "I'm ready."

As she took Quinn's hand in hers, he brought it up to his mouth and breathed on it. "You're so cold."

She leaned into him as he opened the door to the inside, the sounds of merriment escaping from the house.

"I love you," she said before they walked in. "I'm so lucky this is my life and you're going to be my husband."

He squeezed her hand and leaned over to kiss her. "I'm the lucky one."

Quinn held the door open for Meredith and she walked in to find her family and go home.

I hope you enjoyed The Blueberry Bay series! Make sure to check out my many other clean romantic women's fiction series HERE!

If you'd like to receive a FREE standalone novella from my Camden Cove series, please click HERE or visit my website at ellenjoyauthor.com.

# ALSO BY ELLEN JOY

Click HERE for more information about other books by Ellen Joy.

### Cliffside Point

Beach Home Beginnings

Seaview Cottage

Sugar Beach Sunsets

Home on the Harbor

Christmas at Cliffside

Lakeside Lighthouse

Seagrass Sunrise

Half Moon Harbor

Seashell Summer

Beach Home Dreams

### Camden Cove

The Inn by the Cove

The Farmhouse by the Cove

The Restaurant by the Cove

The Christmas Cottage by the Cove

The Bakery by the Cove

### Prairie Valley Sisters

Coming Home to the Valley

Daydreams in the Valley

Starting Over in the Valley

Second Chances in the Valley

New Hopes in the Valley

Feeling Blessed in the Valley

<u>Blueberry Bay</u>

The Cottage on Blueberry Bay

The Market on Blueberry Bay

The Lighthouse on Blueberry Bay

The Fabric Shop on Blueberry Bay

Beach Rose Secrets

# ABOUT THE AUTHOR

Ellen lives in a small town in New England, between the Atlantic Ocean and the White Mountains. She lives with her husband, two sons, and one very spoiled puppy princess.

Ellen writes in the early morning hours before her family wakes up. When she's not writing, you can find her spending time with her family, gardening, or headed to the beach. She loves summer and flip-flops, running on a dirt country road, and a sweet love song.

All of her stories are clean romances where families are close, neighbors are nosy, and the couples are destined for each other.